The Boys Upstairs

The Boys Upstairs

Jane Lebak

Philangelus Press
Boston, MA USA

Other Philangelus Press titles:

The Wrong Enemy
Seven Archangels: Annihilation
Seven Archangels: An Arrow In Flight (Fall, 2014)
Seven Archangels: Sacred Cups (Spring, 2015)

ISBN: 978-1-942133-02-5
eBook ISBN: 978-1-926931-12-8

Cover Art © 2014 by Charlotte Volnek

First edition published by MuseItUp Publishing

For Wendy Dinsmore:

who encouraged me to keep writing this story from the very start, and who loves the characters as much as I do.

"It is a better work to feed the hungry than to raise the dead."

Saint John Chrysostom, 3rd Century Bishop of Constantinople

One

*O*fficer Kevin Farrell took three steps up the walkway before returning to the patrol car. His partner put down the window, and Kevin leaned in. "Maybe this isn't a good idea."

"It's a fine idea." His partner's voice had a *Nothing to see here* depth. "Get your hand off your gun. I doubt you'll get shot down on the front steps of a church."

Kevin looked at his hand as if he hadn't known what it was doing. "Yeah. But for them—" He glanced in the back of the patrol car at three shadowed figures. "I'm not so sure."

"Go!" Bill looked in the back seat. "I'll be waiting here. If you're not out in twenty minutes, I'll come after you, guns a-blazin'."

Kevin snorted. "Do you think it's a sin for a priest to lop off his brother's head?"

The streetlights cast a sparkling glimmer on the two-day-old snow. The church's parking lot was plowed, and the pathway to the rectory shoveled so well that he heard no crunching underfoot. The two-story rectory shone with lights in all the windows. Winter nights darkened early, and Kevin suspected the residents wouldn't settle to sleep for hours still.

At the front door, Kevin waited only a few moments before a boy answered his knock. The kid stood uneasily for several breaths, taking in the policeman's uniform.

"I'm here to see Father Jay Farrell." When the boy didn't move, Kevin took a step around him. "Would you like to go get him, or should I go find him myself?"

The boy blinked rapidly. "I'll get him."

The St. Augustine rectory furnishings were spare, and Kevin's shoes left grit on the threadbare carpet while he stood, arms folded, to the side of the entryway. He'd never been inside before, and the plainness surprised him. Where were the elaborate religious paintings, the deep pile carpet, and the overstuffed furnishings? Or even stuffed furnishings—well, stuffed after 1960. It was clean, but the clean of emptiness, like a home no one had moved into yet. Maybe there was clutter upstairs where the boys lived.

Jay—Father Jay—had a reputation for taking in homeless boys, and now that Kevin thought of it, someone had mentioned that one of the kids seemed a bit slow. Jay wouldn't say it that way, of course. He'd say the kid needed extra processing time.

It was a wonder that with him taking in homeless kids, the rectory hadn't been rifled for stuff they could fence. Although, and with this thought Kevin afforded himself a small smile, there was nothing here to steal. Then he told himself to cool it: it was more than a little uncharitable to be insulting Jay's propensity for taking in homeless kids, given how many months it had been since they'd last spoken. And what he was about to ask.

It took Jay a long time to come to the door, something Kevin accepted without question. When he finally heard steps from the basement, he straightened and moved into the center of the foyer, nearer the light.

As the priest turned the corner, he focused for a long moment before his eyes flared and his breath caught. He took a sharp breath and then limped to the front entrance with a shuffle that even months of physical therapy hadn't erased—but at least there was no indication of pain in his step. It hadn't always been that way. The boy who'd answer the door stuck close to the priest like the Swiss Guard. Two other boys peered down the steps.

Jay squinted at the boys upstairs, and Kevin wondered if he'd noticed their expression of unease in the presence of a police officer.

The cold seeped through the door, and Kevin rubbed his bare hands, looking at them rather than at Jay's habitual squint, his close-cropped black hair and the manner he had of looking directly at the person to whom he spoke. Jay still had his lean, wiry build, but nowadays he had more of the lean than the wiry. Kevin felt bulky and awkward before him, conscious of how Jay had changed from the days they'd raised havoc side by side.

As if he sensed the analysis, Jay turned to Kevin. Without any peripheral vision since his injuries, Jay stared into him like a video camera, and Kevin turned aside.

Jay folded his arms. "What can we do for you, *officer*?"

Officer? Maybe that was just a formality because Jay's boys would spread this exchange all over the street in the next couple of days. Maybe it wouldn't do to have the kids mistrusting Jay because his brother was a cop.

Or maybe Jay was being obtuse, and that was a serve Kevin knew how to return. "Father Farrell," and he made sure to put similar ice into his voice, "I heard you've been housing homeless kids in the rectory. Do you have any room?"

Father Jay Farrell regarded Kevin with an expression he hoped no one, neither the boys nor his brother, could read.

"There's always room for one more," slipped out before he realized that this time, there really wasn't. Currently eight boys lived upstairs, and four of them slept in blankets on the floor. One had no pillow.

"Actually, there's three." Kevin lowered his voice. "We found them in a luggage alcove in the bus station. They need a place to stay."

Jay's expression blanked, and his jaw tightened. "Until you can find them a foster home?"

Kevin shook his head. "They've been in four foster homes already. They're little escape artists, and they want to stay together. If we separate them, they get back together and run away again. We need them all in one place, and I knew you could do that."

Jay rubbed his temples. "Sure, we'll take them in." He couldn't really blame them for wanting to stay together if they were all they had in the world. From what he knew of the public shelters, they were no place for children. Neither were the streets, even when it wasn't five degrees below zero.

As Kevin went to get the kids, admitting a gust of winter, Jay turned to the boys on the stairwell. "Clear out one of the rooms. These kids need to stay together."

One of the boys spoke up. "Where are we going to fit three more?"

"We'll make space for them." Jay's mind combed every inch of the rectory, but no new rooms miraculously appeared on the floor plan. "Even if someone has to sleep on the floor in the boiler room, it's warmer here than outside."

Eddie stood beside Jay, but Jay couldn't read his expression. He laid a hand on Eddie's shoulder. "Go to the kitchen. Heat up some soup."

Kevin escorted in three boys, two of whom hung back behind his legs; one he carried.

Jay looked them over while Kevin tried to get them all inside enough to shut the door. Their breath frosted up, and the middle one had reddened eyes. All of their coats were too small, and none of them had mittens or gloves. Only the littlest wore boots, and even those looked like hand-me-downs. The other two had snow-soaked battered sneakers.

"Come on inside. Let's get you fed." Jay approached, and the two older kids backed against the door. "I'm Father Jay Farrell. You can call me Jay or Father Jay if you want. What are your names?"

After a moment, the oldest said in a small voice, "I'm Louis." He pointed to the littlest one. "That's Jamie."

Jay turned to the middle one. "And you?"

A tiny voice emerged. "Maria."

Jay's heart stilled. He moved up close to Kevin, and with urgency, whispered, "I don't have the facilities to house girls here! There isn't a separate bathroom, and—"

"There's heat and four walls." Kevin shook Jay's hand as if he were an obstetrician congratulating a new dad. "I won't report you."

Jay grabbed Kevin's shoulder, his voice barely louder than a breath. "Can't you find them somewhere else? They'll get eaten alive!"

"What are we supposed to do? Chain them to a radiator at the station house?"

Jay's tone grew dangerous. "It's far better to chain them to a dresser in the rectory?"

There was a silent standoff. Jay looked again at the three smudged faces, the sodden sneakers, and the tangled hair.

"Fine." He sighed. "Let them stay."

"See, that wasn't so hard." Kevin sounded smug. "I knew you'd never refuse me to my face."

"Get out of my church." Jay had long ago perfected a stare that stopped everyone in his tracks, except for his brother, who regarded him with a Teflon smile. "I can't believe you'd drop out of the sky trolling for a favor." He folded his arms. "Stop by tomorrow with some blankets and I may forgive you."

After the door creaked shut behind his brother, Jay escorted the three children up the steps. The rectory's first floor had a standard layout: the parish office, a waiting room, and a conference room. The rectory was designed for four priests, but currently Jay was the only one, and the makeshift basement apartment had seemed the most efficient residence. Before this September, he'd kept the upstairs sealed off to conserve energy. As it had grown colder, though, and the Archangels gang had taken on a couple of homeless boys, he had opened the upper floor for the kids.

Kevin was an idiot. Jay would never have refused those kids no matter who'd brought them.

In the kitchen, chilly even with the heaters banging away, Jay helped the castaways out of their jackets. The girl appeared frostbitten, but she might only have been windblown; her curly blond hair looked chewed-off, as if someone had cropped it close with no care to leave it even. The other two had the same hairstyle, which was why he had assumed she was a boy. While Jay settled them at the table, he asked Eddie to get down bowls and spoons, and also cups. He poured each a glass of milk. Still the children said nothing. Jay took a seat.

"Louis—am I remembering that right? How old are you?"

The boy murmured, "Nine."

The girl looked a couple of years younger. The little one could be no more than four.

Jay said, "The other boys here are a bit older." A mixture of throwaways and runaways, they'd all lived on the streets longer as well. Jay wondered if they would scam on the kids or just show them the ropes and make them appropriately cynical. "The older boys live here because they also have nowhere else to go."

Maria said, "You'll keep us together?"

Jay nodded. "You can stay here together, yes."

Jay told Eddie to take the soup off the stove. Two other boys had shown up in the doorway. "He has to get a job," the taller of the boys said.

"Louis is too young to work. What do you think, Nick? Should I send the four-year-old out to work too?" Jay smiled at the kids, who stared hungrily at the soup Eddie set before them. He said to them, "The older boys have to get jobs to stay. Then they chip in to pay for food and a little rent."

If you could call ten dollars a week rent. Jay all but begged shop-keepers or restaurant owners to take on the boys, who then needed to learn basic job skills such as showing up on time. Some of them bussed tables or helped stack boxes at a grocery store. The boys were working off the books, but Jay didn't worry too much about the law. The law had enough to take care of with the homeless kids resorting to theft and prostitution. As shown by his brother's visit, the police knew what he was doing. They just didn't stop him.

Eddie put some crackers on the table as well. Jay reminded him about the spoons, and after a pause, Eddie brought back five spoons.

Nick snorted. "If the resident idiot doesn't have to work, neither should they."

Jay didn't need to turn to Eddie to know he wouldn't realize the jibe for a moment, and then when he put it together, would get a sick look on his face. Although dealing with physical disability made Jay's life difficult, he suspected mental disability must be much harder, particularly for a homeless boy who needed to survive by his wits.

Turning to Nick and his sharp-eyed smirk, Jay said, "And for that remark, you'll be giving Louis your bed and pillow tonight."

"But—"

Jay sounded placid. "*The Son of Man has nowhere to lay his head*, and now neither do you. Go clear out of that room."

Nick stomped away even as Jay fought the urge to chuckle.

Jay looked at the three kids. He ought to know what to say to them. After all, hadn't his own childhood been a nightmare of gangs, guns and drugs? All that could come to him, though, was, "You'll have a home here as long as you need."

The four-year-old sniffled, and a tear traced down his chapped cheek. Jay reached across the table and put a hand on the boy's shoulder. The little one tensed, but Jay lifted him into his lap and gave him a hug. He shouldn't have done that: even though the boy couldn't have weighed more than forty pounds, it felt as if he'd pulled every muscle in his shoulder.

"We'll take care of you," Jay said.

The boy looked at his lap. "But how is Santa Claus going to find us?"

Two

*B*ill pulled away from the curb while Kevin radioed to say they had dropped off the kids. As he set the radio back on the hook, Bill said, "How'd you know he'd take them?"

"He can't say no. He's got a whole zoo in there." Kevin laughed. "He's even got a little gang of kids that protects the parish. They call themselves the Archangels."

Bill did a double-take. He was a tall black man, well-muscled and imposing in his uniform when he wanted to be. "I've heard about them. They're his?"

"He caught a bunch of kids brawling in the parking lot one night and somehow got them to not only stop fighting, but to leave their older brothers' gangs. I have no idea what he said to them. But you know how it is: they just formed a new gang, and they call the church their territory." Kevin shrugged. "They said the bishop had five kinds of fits."

With a laugh, Bill said, "I can imagine!"

In a slightly off-key voice, Kevin sang to the tune of *Jesus Christ Is Risen Today*, "Jay's in trouble with the bishop again. How surprising!"

Bill snorted. "What's his deal? I like kids, so I got married and had three. You'd think if he liked kids that much, he wouldn't have become a priest."

"I don't think he likes kids. At least, he didn't." Kevin adjusted the patrol car's heater. "Maybe it's penance or karma or something. He was a little hooligan himself."

"Is that how he got shot up?"

"No. Gulf war."

"You're kidding! Army?"

"Yep."

"Chaplain?"

Kevin barked a laugh. "Not hardly. You know how you just know which kids on the street corners are only a nuisance and which are going on to become career perps? He was going that way fast." Kevin laughed. "Heck, I was too! We were 'Farrell and His Shadow', a pair of hell-raisers, but he was always the one in the lead, coming up with ridiculous stunts, telling me what to do, introducing me to all sorts of things he shouldn't have, just like a big brother."

Bill slapped his leg. "I knew there was more to you, man!"

"Really?" Kevin paused. "Well, my dad worked like a thousand hours a week. He didn't care what we did, as long as he didn't have to get called into the school or into the station house."

Bill shook his head.

"It surprised the dickens out of everyone when Jay enlisted." Kevin swallowed. "Me too. I didn't even know he'd been talking to the recruiting guy. Then Jay went to Iraq and came home half-dead." Kevin took a deep breath. "He got all weird on us, always talking about God and reading his Bible. He became Catholic, and then two years later he went into the seminary. I kept hoping they'd kick him out because he's nearly blind, but no."

Bill sat straighter. "You'd rather he was a career perp than a priest?"

"I'm not sure which one I'd prefer." Kevin's mouth twitched. "I can't say which view of the world is more twisted. Either you're out there taking what you can because you're stronger than everyone, or else you're taking what you can because God told you to do it."

Bill pulled onto the main strip. "Bitter much, Kevin?"

Kevin snorted. "What's God ever done for him?"

"Apparently saved his life and kept him from spending eighty years in the lockup."

"Sent him to the poorest inner-city church there is." Kevin looked out the side window. "He's wasting his life."

"That's why you went from being his shadow to not talking to him more than twice a year?"

"It's awful to see what my own brother's doing to himself. And all for a lie."

When Bill didn't respond, Kevin looked back at him. "This world is a nasty place that doesn't give anyone any second chances. I told you what happened to my mother. Some drunk driver comes out of nowhere, and there's no second chance for her. How many times have we found kids who tried to smoke the latest thing for the first time and ended up dead? No second chance for them either. People made up God so they'd have someone else to blame for all the random garbage life throws their way. Then they could say they'd have a second chance in the next world. And my brother bought right into it when life threw garbage at him. Sorry. It doesn't hold any water for me."

Bill didn't look at all disturbed. "I suppose I shouldn't tell you I believe in God, then?"

"Believe what you like, man." Kevin nodded toward the expensive sports number in front of them. "Hey, have you noticed how that car keeps bucking, like the guy hasn't ever driven a stick-shift before?"

"You mean the Audi TT I've been tailing for the last half-mile? Yeah, I think it's time we pull him over and find out it's stolen. Hit the lights."

Holly Mayfield came into her dark kitchenette to find the answering machine blinking. It was so old that the triangle had worn off the 'play' button. While the tape whined on the spools, she removed her coat and gloves, set her hat on the tabletop, and glanced at the microwave. One o'clock in the morning. Her shift hadn't been as bad tonight as it could have been. At least there hadn't been any customers entering the restaurant ten minutes before closing asking to be seated and served a full dinner. On the other hand, three tables had only tipped her a dollar each on their tickets, and she'd had one walk-out.

Her mother was on the message machine, reminding her that Aunt Mary's birthday was next week, and that she should send a card. The other message was Father Jay, asking if she had any extra blankets or pillows because he'd just acquired three additional children.

"You know," Holly said to herself as she walked into the living room, "some people collect normal things, like stamps or coins. You collect kids."

She happened to have two beat-up old pillows in a closet for when her brother came to town. They used to be her "real" pillows, but last year they'd finally gotten flatter than the inside of a band-aid, and she'd retired them. Her brother put both in the same pillowcase, declaring it fine because together they about made one pillow. She hoped the kids wouldn't mind, since the alternative was nothing. Did Father Jay even have pillowcases for them? Probably not. She sighed.

She had one extra blanket, again the one she saved for her brother. Her brother wouldn't be visiting this Christmas, so she could send it over to the rectory too. She used an old throw when she watched TV, but now that the restaurant had her working night shifts she didn't watch much, so that could go. The third kid—well, God had better provide, because she couldn't.

It scared her that Father Jay had called for help. When he reached for the phone, it meant he had his back to the wall. Saying there were no pillows and blankets left at the rectory meant he was sleeping with his head on a folded t-shirt and the rest of him under his winter coat.

Ah, now if only he had a brother...I mean, a brother I could date. Holly hung her coat in the hall closet, and set her purse on the hook, and then slipped out of her shoes and left them in front of the shoe rack. *God, you've got to do something about Kevin.* After Jay's introduction during a church get-together last year, she had gone on two dates with Kevin. He had Jay's bearing in a way Holly imagined Jay would have if he hadn't gotten injured, although more handsome than Jay, more muscular and more apt to laugh at her silly jokes. Kevin and Jay shared a tendency to suddenly satirize a familiar song, but neither could carry a tune. Kevin could make her laugh. Unfortunately, Kevin had such an open hostility toward religion that Holly declined a third invitation to go out with him. It was a shame.

In the bedroom, Holly pulled free her hair clip, then dumped all the change and crumpled bills from her pockets onto her dresser. It made a nice pile. She could pretend it contained treasure that would leave her comfortably shopping for groceries and then taking a trip to the mall for lavish Christmas presents for her family. In reality, it was always just enough to keep her squeaking by. She counted herself lucky that a fifteen percent tip at this restaurant was a living wage. At the last one, customers tipped on smaller checks, so for the same number of trips to the tables, she ended up taking home far less.

She stacked the coins, sorted the bills, totaled it out, and wrote the amount in her notebook. Before going to bed she managed to make a roll of dimes and two rolls of pennies. The quarters she kept in a mayonnaise jar for doing laundry. While rolling coins, she prayed, *Dear God, thank you for a good night tonight. Thank you for letting me get out of there before two o'clock in the morning. And please be sure to bless that nice couple who tipped me twenty bucks. I didn't even really do anything special for them.*

Her mouth twitched. *And I guess I'm supposed to pray for that jerk who commented about how I looked in my uniform and then ended up tipping me a dollar when I refused to go out with him. I dunno—maybe you could give him a conscience or something?* She grinned. *At the very least, please take care of Father Jay and those boys he keeps upstairs. He has no idea what he's in for with all of them, has he?*

Kevin opened his locker to retrieve his duffle bag. The heavy belt weighted down his waist, but he didn't remove it. He took off first his shirt, then his bullet-proof vest, then replaced his shirt, and grabbed his jacket.

Christmas songs. Christmas lights. Christmas trees. Only a little longer until the gifts were exchanged (both with one another and at the stores) and the trees went to the curbside. The songs would play for a few more days, and then it would be over. Red and pink would go up for Valentine's Day, and the world would go back to normal. Christmas was only one day, but it had expanded to fill an entire sixth of the year.

Two years ago, Kevin had been joking with his then-partner in the patrol car when they'd gotten a call for a domestic. Routine for Christmas Eve— unfortunately, domestic violence rocketed around town like Santa on his sleigh at Christmas time. Always disgusting, but the character of the holiday threw the violence into sharper relief. Men beating their wives because they'd cooked the turkey wrong: joy to the world.

Kevin and his partner had just finished up when they got a call about a car accident. They responded with sirens screaming, racing down the centerline of the boulevard as cars dived to the curbs. He arrived to find two cars mangled together like lovers shot by a jealous husband. A Ford Taurus on its back, the side caved in, and a Camry impacted so hard on the driver's side it was bent like an L. A third sedan, make and model unidentifiable, had its engine in the front seat, smashed head-on into a wall.

Running through the glass shards that crunched like ice beneath his steel-toed shoes, Kevin went to the Camry and shone his flashlight through the shatter-frosted window to see there was no way to help this woman. His partner checked the flipped Taurus, and again, nothing.

Kevin would have bet the house drugs were involved. Instead, the autopsy results came back clean. Just a driver racing to the mall.

Jobs that should never be done: calling the coroner on Christmas Eve. More than that: being the one to contact a dead driver's family the night before Christmas. He'd managed to secure the contents of one car for the family so they'd have at least this final Christmas gift.

Such a senseless crash, an act of stupid haste and three lives snuffed like a smoldering candle. Kevin would remember forever crunching up two icy steps on a wooden porch entwined with blinking white lights, a push of the doorbell, and the terror flashing across a middle-aged woman's face as she opened the door to a police officer. "Are you Mrs. Sherry Daniels?"

What more do you say after that? How do you make the unbearable able to be borne?

Next November, Kevin recoiled the first time he saw porches adorned with blinking white lights. It took two weeks to figure out why. He went to the Daniels family's house on Christmas Eve that year— no blinking lights, not then—carrying a plant and a sympathy card. They weren't home, so Kevin left them on the steps. This year he wouldn't go at all. He'd mentally kicked himself over and over for not considering the mother's reaction if she'd been there, if she'd seen him on a second Christmas Eve.

He never came to bring glad tidings of great joy, that's for sure. That was why everyone in the city either hated the cops or feared them. Kevin looked at himself in the mirror some mornings and thought, *That's me. Someone to be hated and feared.*

As he put his cap back into his locker, Kevin caught sight of the metal inside the brim, or rather the medal. Jay had given it to him when he'd entered the police academy, insisted he pin it somewhere on the uniform, and a lot of cops had the same one. A medal of Saint Michael. Kevin knew from the wings that Michael was an angel, not why he would be the patron of police officers. *Do you ever manage to do any good,* he thought to the angel figure, *or does everyone hate and fear you too?*

That was something Jay maybe understood, if Kevin ever felt like asking. Although Kevin couldn't say for certain, he figured priests too must be hated and feared. Feared as if they were judges or magicians, hated because they represented the Church and everything it stood for in the minds of everyone on Earth. Like the police, priests were meant to be trusted, access to a law higher than the citizenry, and so often unable to enforce a damned thing. Jay couldn't stop a man from sinning, and Kevin couldn't stop a young woman from dying on Christmas Eve.

He slammed his locker and sighed.

One of the other guys looked up. "Long night?"

"I hate Christmas."

"Ho ho ho. Merry paperwork." The guy laughed, but Kevin only left the locker room to head for home.

Half an hour driving, listening to talk radio in his car, and watching the digital clock during light cycles. Once home, he locked away his gun and set aside his uniform. In front of the TV he flipped channels until he found a movie with lots of explosions, then left it running in the background as he changed into flannel pajama pants and grabbed a bag of chips. The recliner creaked as he settled himself. He checked his voicemail, one message.

Dad's scratchy voice. "I didn't want to call later, in case you're sleeping."

Kevin rolled his eyes. *I'm on a night tour, Dad— figure it out.*

"I wasn't sure what your off days would be for the rest of the week. They've got a full schedule for Christmas Eve and Christmas Day, so I may not be able to catch you over the holiday. If I don't get a chance to talk to you, have a merry Christmas."

"You too," Kevin said to the voicemail. "You and five hundred other retirees in a gated Florida community." He leaned back in front of the TV set. "Don't do anything I wouldn't do."

The movie was boring, loud, and predictable. Kevin woke up an hour later to find it had already ended. He shut off the set and dragged himself to bed. Two more days until Christmas.

Three

$\mathcal{D}$ivine providence didn't have to alert Jay when the trio of newcomers tried to escape. The old rectory creaked with as many different tones as a symphony orchestra, and having been an escape artist himself as a teen, Jay knew what to expect.

And so it was that when Louis, Maria and Jamie got to the front door, one stuffed-full pillowcase in Maria's arms and Jamie in Louis's, Jay met them there.

"It's really too cold to leave in the middle of the night." He gestured toward the parlor as the three children clustered together in fear. "I'd never spank you, and I know I can't keep you if you're determined to go. But if you have to leave, you might as well leave in the morning."

The kids shuffled into the parlor alongside the front entrance, and Jay turned on the lights so they could make their way onto the couch. He sat in a chair across the room.

"Why are you leaving?"

They stared at him with three sullen pouts.

Jay said, "I'm not a foster home here. The boys who live upstairs moved in because it was a warm place to stay. Most of them ran away from home too, or were thrown out." He waited. "Where are you from?"

Louis answered, and Jay recognized the neighborhood, a twenty-minute drive from here. He asked if they had any family. They all looked at one another, and then Louis said no, they didn't.

Ah: so they did have family, but no one to take them in.

He asked if they went to school. Louis said sometimes. He asked if they liked school, and it turned out they did, kind-of.

Through all this, the kids looked at one another before answering, and Jamie never said anything at all. The youngest, he dozed against Louis's shoulder.

Maria looked right at him, frowning. "We don't want a new dad."

Jay raised his hands. "I'm not anyone's dad. In the Church, priests are called Father, but I'm not anyone's father."

There was a moment of quiet before Louis said, "And no new mom, either."

He nodded.

Maria said, "Why are you doing this, then? Is it for the money?"

Dear God, why did little ones have to get so cynical? He assured them that he received no money for having them in the house, nor did he want any.

"But you're crippled," Louis said "So how are you getting money?"

Cynical and no punches pulled; an excellent combination for life on the street. "I'm a priest. The diocese pays me, and I do work for them."

Maria said, "But if we run, you can't catch us."

He shook his head.

"How'd you get hurt?" Louis said.

"I used to be a soldier. I was in Iraq, and I got hurt there."

Louis sat forward. "A real soldier? Like you carried a gun and wore a uniform? Like GI Joe?"

Jay nodded. "Except I didn't have all that cool gear and neat code names like they do."

Louis said, "And did the enemy shoot you?"

Jay hesitated.

Ten years ago, a shattered army division had returned to base in a wrecked jeep with four of its soldiers barely alive. They'd driven over a land mine. A medical team had begun treatment the moment they'd stopped the vehicle, and shortly the wounded were transported to a combat support hospital. Within the hour the doctors passed the word back to their commanding officer that one had already died and the rest wouldn't survive the night.

The other three died before sunrise. Only Jay had survived.

"Did it hurt?" Maria said.

Louis shoved her. "Of course it hurt, idiot! He got shot bad enough to cripple him!"

Opting against explaining about ballistics, explosives and the more graphic parts of war, Jay said, "I was unconscious for a week, actually, so it didn't hurt at first. Later on, yeah."

He'd been airlifted to Germany, where he stayed in a coma fourteen days. At every turn, the doctors had said, "We can try this procedure, but he most likely won't survive it," and then they'd tried and he'd survived. But when they'd said he'd most likely have very little vision and no motion in either leg, that time they'd been correct. When Jay awoke, he couldn't see at all from his left eye, the right one unfocused spontaneously, and he was paralyzed from the waist down. At first his hands trembled so badly he couldn't write or hold a cup. It took another week to get him off the respirator.

Louis said, "You weren't a priest back then?"

Jay nodded. "I didn't even believe in God back then. *God* was just something I said when I was mad."

Maria said, "When did you become a priest?"

"Not until years later."

Recovery had been so, so slow. Over time the tremors eased, the vision improved, and his strength returned. There had been physical therapy, tests, more tests, endless days in a hospital bed with a TV he couldn't see, medications that made him unable to think, and time. Lots and lots of time.

Louis said, "So you went back to the war?"

"I couldn't. I wasn't able to drive, I couldn't see, and I couldn't stand. I couldn't even read except by focusing on one letter at a time." Jay sounded rueful. "If they'd put a gun into my hands, who knows what

I'd have shot? The army sent me to a hospital in America."

Maria said, "And then what?"

Jay let out a long breath. "Well--"

But these were kids. Telling this story to adults often made them say something tolerant like, "That's nice," or Kevin's, "You've got to be shitting me!" But kids tended to trust in the bizarre. Would this cut through their cynicism, or would they also think he was lying?

"I hated it in the hospital," Jay said. "I didn't want to talk to anyone. I hated the doctors, hated the nurses. I just wanted to leave."

Louis sat forward, shifting Jamie on his lap. "Yeah!"

Oh, right, Louis felt like a caged tiger too. Jay nodded in response to his enthusiasm. "I wished I could escape, but I couldn't. Even if I left, I was stuck with myself."

Louis and Maria were looking him dead in the face, waiting. Jamie snored lightly on Louis's shoulder.

"One day I heard some kids playing in the hallway. It sounded like they were saying, 'Take and read,' but they were really saying 'one-two-three.'" He chuckled. "It was annoying me until I thought, 'Maybe I really should take and read something, it's better than sitting here.' Someone from the hospital had left me a copy of *The Lives of the Saints*. They told a story about one hero for every day of the year, so I picked the hero for my birthday."

Maria said, "Like firefighters and baseball players?"

"It was a different heroism," Jay said. "The hero I found was a soldier, and he'd been injured just like me. His name was Ignatius Loyola."

Louis was almost bouncing on the couch, Jamie bumping against him. "What did he do?"

Jay told them about Ignatius Loyola, how he was so vain that when he saw his broken leg was set crooked, he'd had his leg broken again to re-set it, and how during recovery he'd changed his mind and become a soldier for God instead; how he'd founded a group that sent priests wherever they were needed all over the world. He told them how another injured soldier had changed the world.

Because that night, Jay had been just as enthralled. He didn't get any sleep at all as he devoured the chapter one letter at a time, and then the next. By the end of August he had finished the entire volume, and several days later, steeling himself, he picked up the Bible. Again he opened at random. He read Mark 3:13.

"Jesus went up the mountain and summoned those whom he wanted, and they came to him."

Jay had shut the book and lain still for an hour.

Louis said, "He just called anyone he wanted, and they came?"

Jay nodded. "Just like that."

Maria said, "No one ever wanted us. They wish we'd never been born."

"I want you here," said Jay.

Ten years ago, that had been the first time he'd thought anyone had wanted him, too. Wounded and damaged, he'd had no more use in this world. His old friends had forgotten him. His family visited so infrequently that he could hear the renewed pain in their voices every time they saw him, as if they forgot between visits that fate had done the equivalent of running his life through a lawn mower. The army couldn't use him any longer.

By extension, God didn't need him to do anything—Jay knew that by rights he ought to have died in the Jeep. But what he'd just read belied that: God called those he wanted, not those he needed. And maybe, just maybe, Jay had survived for a reason. Maybe because he was wanted.

"And that's why you're here now," Jay said. "If God called you and you came, I'm not sending you away. Even if God called and you didn't hear it, you're with me now. If you try to escape, you can always come back. But for now, I need to ask you to stay, at least until the sun's up and it's a bit warmer out there."

Maria and Louis looked at one another.

"Can you do that for me?" Jay said.

Louis nodded. Maria consented as well.

"Then go back upstairs and get some sleep," Jay said. "I'll show you around the church in the morning, and you can decide if you want to stay after all."

Four

Jay shut off the alarm clock fifteen minutes before it would have rung on December 23rd. The lineup of *things to do* stretched before him like a thousand car freight train, and his brain kept reviewing it all. By 5:00 he had showered, and now he stood in his kitchen waiting for the coffee to brew. The drops emerged from the percolator one at a time, and he squinted at the coffee uneasily. His heavy glasses still didn't make the image clear. He'd realize when the coffee finished by the sound of the steam, but he watched anyhow.

Eventually he'd have to give up coffee. At four dollars a pound, he could hardly justify the luxury much longer. Last year, Lent had coincided with the day he'd run out of coffee, so he'd clenched his teeth and called it a sign from God. Holly must have sensed, somehow, because on Easter morning she'd arrived with a gift from the Easter Bunny, enough coffee to keep him stocked through summer. He shouldn't have taken it, knowing how hard she worked, but with that practical insistence of hers, she'd forced him. Looking at the coffee pot now, he had the sinking feeling of a guilty pleasure. He was pretty sure God was asking him to give up coffee because every time he thought about it, he tried to come up with a way out.

Pushing the glasses back up onto the bridge of his nose, he smirked. The coffee and the contact lenses—those were the last two big expenses he ought to eliminate from his budget. He'd never had much faith in budgets, and he'd laughed when they made him take a business administration course in seminary, but he really needed it running this parish. His tendency would have been to add up all the expenses at the end of the year and pretend those were his projections to begin with, but the diocese didn't allow it.

This church was too poor to make the numbers work. Jay had taken his diocesan salary, pathetic as it might be, and thrown more than half of it into the parish's income column. That put Jay's personal income well under five figures, but sacrifice got easier once he started translating the dollars into pounds of rice or beans or spaghetti. During the difficult moments, Jay tried to imagine the fifteen or twenty faces who would be denied food so he could have coffee, more heat, or a longer shower. (No one had ever noticed the bell timer in the bathroom, thank goodness.)

The soup kitchen put them in the red nearly every month. It didn't matter. He always found a way. After staring down Iraqi gun-barrels, he wasn't about to let a little addition and subtraction stop him.

Jay dragged his thoughts back to the immediate problems of today, December 23rd. Laundry was just as easy now as it had been in the army: Jay had gone from one profession to another where he seldom had to decide what to wear in the morning. The black clothes, unfortunately, required ironing, and that he had to take care of before he could start the day.

Shortly after Jay began ironing, the window slid up and a scrawny blond boy wriggled through, admitting a blast of wind. Jay didn't turn his head. "Hi, Masa."

"Hey, man, help me out." Masa dropped his book bag on the floor and started unbuttoning his shirt. "The headmaster said if I showed up all wrinkled one more time, I'm suspended, and Mom didn't iron nothing anyhow. It's only a half day before Christmas break, so she said it didn't matter."

Jay finished a black shirt while Masa handed him his smaller white one "And that would be a shame, after how many people we begged to get you a scholarship."

"You won't have to beg nobody next year, though. We get report cards today. I think I'm going to get an A in English, man!" Masa grinned. "You saw last semester I got all Bs and Cs. I never got a C before!"

Jay looked at him sidelong to catch that moment of embarrassed delight in the boy's eyes. While smart, Masa had never applied himself in grammar school. Jay had pulled enough strings to get him admitted to the local Catholic middle school, but the admissions board had been understandably wary: he'd had over a hundred absences the year before. The second chance was paying off. With only ten absences so far, Masa might well get a free ride next year. A few other Archangels already attended the middle school, and Masa had started a chapter over there, policing the school grounds much as the first group patrolled the church.

Jay looked at the boy sitting on the steps adjusting his red armband. "Should you be wearing a gang emblem to school?"

"Who's going to take it off me?"

Jay tossed Masa the warm, pressed shirt. "I was thinking about the faculty. Make sure you get the bus on time."

"Yeah." Masa stopped buttoning his shirt to think a minute. "You know, you'd have been a cool dad."

"I am a dad," Jay said as Masa let himself back outside through the basement window. "I've got all you guys."

Plus a gal. *We really need to find a place for those kids. They can't stay here.* What an ugly, fallen world, if small children had to face homelessness or separation. *Oh, God, just let them be safe until we find them a decent place.*

And decent food. And warm clothes without holes.

Jay checked his watch. Maybe Kevin was home now—and if so, he was definitely still asleep. Waking him with a phone call would be decidedly unchristian, but Jay took a momentary satisfaction in imagination. "It's six o'clock in the morning, and I still have two kids sleeping on wood floors upstairs with no blanket and no pillows. What's that? You say I rousted you out of your warm full-size bed in your heated second story apartment with the balcony and the wall-to-wall carpeting?"

Ah, yes. Shades of the best his childhood had to offer, but no, he'd call Kevin later. It would help to know if the kids had any belongings they could scavenge, if Kevin could look into their previous foster homes and find some toiletries. Did they even have any toys? Maybe a stuffed animal would make the nights less lonely for the youngest two. Maybe their previous caretakers had never bothered with that kind of stuff.

The powerless are the ones who suffer when there's not enough to go around, God, and no one's more powerless than our children. The Gospels talked about Jesus taking a small child on his lap and saying the kingdom of heaven belonged to children like this. Children like Nick, furious at the injustice of the world; children like Maria whose parents had abandoned them; children like Masa, denied the resources for a decent start in life. Children like Eddie, who wanted to succeed so badly and were never given even a first chance.

Thursday was grocery day, and with eleven homeless kids to feed, Jay wondered if he could get all of the necessary items into the trunk of a car. He didn't own a vehicle because the municipal government frowned on legally blind people driving, but since Holly worked second shift she had volunteered to drive him weekly for groceries, tithing out of her time what she couldn't from income.

This morning, Holly only laughed as she unloaded a couple of blankets, pillows and towels from the back seat of her beat-up compact. "Maybe next time I should bring your brother's police van instead."

As they drove, Holly said, "Tell me what you want for Christmas."

Jay shrugged. "I don't want anything."

"You live on a handful of change a week, and this is an excuse to get you one of the luxury items you refuse to buy yourself." Holly wore a no-nonsense look that usually tamed the boys upstairs. "So don't give me the 'I don't want anything' routine. You're going to get something. It might as well be something you want."

"The parish office could use—"

"For Pete's sake, Jay!" Holly pulled into a Burger-Haven drive-through. "Let God figure out how to get the parish office more canary yellow typing paper or an extra box of staples. I'm talking about you. You. Jay." She stuck her head out the window and called to the drive-through speaker, "Big Topper junior meal with a small diet cola." She looked at Jay. "You want anything?"

"Nothing."

She put her head back out the window. "One Big Topper extra value meal with a cola, and super-size the fries."

As Holly idled to the window, Jay said, "I was wondering why you even bother asking me."

"Because someday you'll get tired of me guessing what you'd like and guessing wrong."

"That's going to backfire if I honestly have no preference, of course."

"That's not the point. What I want is to help. I'm not going to break your vow of poverty by getting you a Christmas gift. Just tell me what you need. You're the only person I could give something to and know it matters."

Holly paid for the meal, handed Jay the paper bag, and pulled out onto the road again. Jay ate quickly. While he didn't dwell on it, he had felt hungry.

Holly huffed. "You all but bleed to save everyone else's life. Why are you making my life difficult?"

Jay said, "A can opener."

Holly glanced his way. "A can opener."

Jay shook his head. "No, not a regular can opener. You know, the kind you plug in."

"An electric can opener."

"Right."

"I'll get you a can opener on the way home. What do you want for *Christmas*?"

"Up until a minute ago," Jay said with amusement, "I thought I wanted a can opener."

"But that's—"

"You asked what I could use. Sometimes it hurts my hands to turn the regular one."

Holly breathed sharply. Jay couldn't make out the expression on her face, but he imagined her silence was a horrified one. She made such a little issue out of his disabilities that sometimes he imagined she forgot them entirely. "I'll get it for you. But I have to get you more than that."

Jay fixed a pointed gaze on her. "Okay. Then give me a totally non-commercial Christmas. Give me a holiday where people haven't forgotten the 'Holy' in the middle of skittering hither and yon to find thirty-five of that perfect gift, color-coordinating their wrapping paper with their living-room decor, igniting seventy-five thousand watts of Christmas Spirit on their front lawn, and creating choirs of store-owners gathered around their cash registers singing 'What A Friend We Have In Jesus.'"

Holly didn't answer. Jay huffed.

A half mile down the road, Jay said, "What does your restaurant do with the leftover bread at the end of the day?"

"We toss most of it. Sometimes the kitchen staff takes it home. The manager is pretty tight and we usually don't have much."

"The Archangels said that Gino's bakery isn't having as much left over at the end of the day any longer. We've been counting on bread donations to keep the soup kitchen running for a while now, and the boys eat like crazy." Jay took a deep breath. "Could you ask about the expired food and day-old bread? They'd get the tax write-off, and we'd get some more people fed. I was hoping you could persuade them to help out."

Holly laughed. "Because I'm such a high-powered individual there?"

"Because they're decent human beings?"

"I wouldn't go that far." Holly shrugged. "Donations are way down?"

"It's the Christmas spirit. Everyone's picking out plastic singing toys to drop in the collection bins at the Salvation Army. But the poor still need to eat."

So, apparently, did everyone else. The grocery store parking lot was filled out to the very last spaces. Holly dropped off Jay at the front entrance while she went to park in what she referred to as the "north 40." Standing beside a mailbox, Jay listened to snippets of conversations. Most walked in alone, shopped alone, and returned home alone. More than three couples were arguing about their menus as they entered the store, and several moms were having a hard time corralling their children. Jay smothered a smile as one mom reminded her daughter to use her "shopping manners."

He squinted at the advertisements, printed huge enough that even he could read them. Shrimp a bargain at $6.99 a pound, cuts of prime rib that cost thirty dollars on sale. "Get a free turkey with a purchase of $150." *Actually, that may not be a bad idea. I wonder if I could get someone to roast a turkey for the kids upstairs. I wonder if that oven actually works. You can't microwave a turkey, can you?*

Holly arrived, her gloved hands shoved into her pockets. "Let's get started. You should have waited inside where it's warmer."

"Is it possible to microwave a turkey?"

As the automatic doors slid open, Holly said, "Right now I'd crawl inside the microwave with it."

After they finished grocery shopping, Holly packed the car, and Jay scanned the parking lot. It wouldn't pay to approach this store's manager again, especially on a day when the man had already wrestled (figuratively—Jay hoped) so many irate customers, scammers and folks who wanted to use expired coupons, unverified checks, or maxed credit cards. He'd actually seen one manager called over to deal with a customer who simply "wanted a discount." No other reason. Just, "I want a discount."

Jay had already worked over as many of the local proprietors as he could, trying to find jobs for the boys. So many times when he entered a business, he received the same dour look, the blankness, the unthinking denial.

No doubt any request for a job would be met with, "Are you nuts?"

But maybe he should try again. For Eddie's sake, maybe he should give it one more shot.

If nobody will give these boys a job because they're not good in the eyes of the world, how can they become good in the eyes of the world? His own wild youth seemed so different. At least his family had been intact, a warm place to sleep at whatever hour of the morning he'd returned home. He didn't pry into their pasts, but Jay assumed he'd done far worse than the kids he housed now. Certainly with less excuse. He'd been almost feral, arrested twice for petty theft, possessing a weapon and DUI, always let off the hook by his father's connections. He'd refused to attend college, instead enlisting in the Army just in time for the Gulf War where he had driven his truck over a land mine. Praise God for land mines.

Five

"Thank goodness," Jay said as Holly pulled in to the church parking lot. "Kevin's car. I hope he brought sleeping bags for the kids."

Holly parked. "Did he say he would?"

"Not exactly."

"What did he say, *exactly*?"

"I think he *exactly* said, 'Do you have any idea what time it is?' It was eight in the morning. I told him he missed a beautiful sunrise."

Holly choked on a laugh.

Jay started to unload the groceries but was stopped momentarily by three of the older boys who pushed him out of the way. "Try not to eat it all before it gets into the fridge," he called after them as they competed to see which of them could haul the largest number of bags up the stairs at the same time. Holly hid her mouth in her hands as she laughed.

Kevin came out of his car and joined them. "The church secretary said you would be back around now."

"Mrs. D. knows all," Jay said. "What did you bring the boys?"

"A couple of the guys from the precinct went to the kids' group home last night and found some clothes for them and a couple of toys, some stuffed animals. They didn't have much, but you've got some bedding now at least." Kevin shook his head. "When they got removed from their parents, apparently there was no food in the cabinets and only four pillows for the five of them, but a widescreen TV and a stereo surround sound system."

Holly's eyes widened. "What kind of priorities are those?"

Jay stared at a crack in the pavement. "I think it's clear where the priority was."

"Crystal clear," said Kevin. "I could tell you all about women who show up at the station house asking for help because they can't afford to buy food this week, but they have their nails done and their hair permed, and their nine-year-old girl is walking in behind them with her nails done and her hair permed too."

Jay flinched. "I don't suppose you talk to them about budgeting?"

"Not my problem," Kevin said. "It's not breaking the law to spend your money on useless crap."

"Send them to me," Jay said. "I'll at least get them a meal."

Kevin shook his head. "Sometimes I wonder what it takes for people to come to their senses."

"Land mines?" Jay shook his head. "The Cafeteria is here until that happens." He squinted at Kevin. "Did you bring the kids' things inside?"

"Not yet. I figured it would make the kids nervous to see an off-duty cop going into their rooms."

"True. Nick can spot a cop fifty miles away." Jay glanced at Holly, but then he didn't say anything.

"I'll keep you posted on the kids, if anything turns up." Kevin paused. "I've got someone working on getting the rectory listed as an emergency foster care house. You'd get some money from that, at any rate."

"Will they have to come in and inspect?"

"I took care of that."

Jay rolled his eyes.

Kevin laughed. "Don't worry about it. There's a need and you're meeting it. Good to see you again, Holly."

"You too."

As Kevin retrieved the kids' belongings, Holly said, "I'll need to be going now. I'm opening today."

"He's still available, you know."

She shook her head. "He's not really available."

"I keep telling you that hostility toward God is still contact with Him." Jay grinned at her. "No one would be that angry if God wasn't working on his heart. Think of it as his last defense against God."

She cocked her head. "I seem to remember the Bible telling us not to be unevenly yoked."

"I have no choice about being unevenly yoked—he's my brother." Jay sighed. "Besides, if you were married to him, you'd be looking after him rather than me."

"I thought Paul wrote that the unmarried woman is after the concerns of the Lord?"

Jay rubbed his chin. "You'll notice that Paul never said that was a good thing."

Her jaw dropped. "Ooh, you're mean. See if you get your can opener for Christmas."

"Woe is me!" Jay laid his hand over his heart. "Held hostage by a can opener. *What good is it to save the whole world, but to lose my can opener?*"

While Holly was laughing, Kevin returned with two black garbage bags. "You ready, Jay?"

Holly rubbed her gloved hands together. "I'll ask about the bread today."

She went back to her car, and Jay labored up the snow-dusted steps to the rectory, Kevin a step behind.

Eddie was sitting at the table with a peanut-butter sandwich when Nick stalked into the kitchen. "Shove over. You're taking up too much space, Retard."

Eddie pulled his glass of milk closer to his plate, then moved his napkin closer as well. Nick shoved the jar of peanut butter so it knocked into the milk, sloshing it up by the top of the glass. Eddie said nothing.

Nick opened the cupboard and stared at it until finally pulling out a box of cereal and pouring it into a white mug with a faded logo. Then he grabbed the container of milk and a spoon to eat standing by the counter.

"You got a job yet, Retard?"

Eddie looked down. "Um, no."

"You going to look for a job?"

"Father Jay said—"

"Does Father Jay wipe your mouth for you too after you eat? You've got to work or you're getting kicked out." Nick grinned. "Father Jay said I can have your bed and your pillow if you don't find a job by Christmas."

Eddie looked worried. "I didn't know that. I've tried. No one wants me."

"Got that right." Nick ate some more cereal and then frowned at him over the top of the mug. "Maybe you could get a job at the zoo shoveling up after the elephants. No, that would be too hard for you, wouldn't it? Require too much brain power."

"Lay off," said Louis, coming into the kitchen. "You're always such a jerk."

Behind him came Maria and Jamie.

Nick rolled his eyes and stepped out of the way of the two little ones, standing over Eddie's seat. "You're just a loser and no one wants you around. I bet that's why you got kicked out of your home."

Louis said, "Then why'd you get the boot, Nick?"

But Eddie was already answering. "My mom left. They told me to go too. They said if she wasn't there, I couldn't be there either."

"That rots," said Louis.

Nick snorted. "Why'd your mom leave? Did you stink up the place too bad for her to stay?"

"Excuse me, Nick," said the deep voice of Father Jay, "but I won't tolerate harassment in this rectory."

Nick went back to shoveling cereal into his mouth.

"We have house rules for a reason." Father Jay glanced at Eddie, who was looking forlornly at his peanut-butter sandwich. "This house is a safe place for all of you. I'm not having you make it unsafe."

Nick slammed his empty mug and spoon onto the table. "Fine. Whatever."

Father Jay grabbed his arm as he tried to push past out of the kitchen. "In the sink. You know that."

Nick turned back, dropped the mug in with a clatter, and then stalked away.

"It's okay." Louis put a hand on Eddie's' shoulder. "Nick's like that to everyone."

Jay turned to Kevin, who was standing behind him. "It's hard to let go of the street even in here."

Maria and Jamie were looking up at Kevin, frowning. Jay remembered that the last time they'd seen his brother, he was wearing a uniform.

In a low voice, Kevin said, "You can't change a kid."

"You can change everything around him and let God change the kid." Jay took a seat beside Eddie, and a moment later Jamie was climbing into his lap. "What's up?"

Another boy, one with the unfortunate nickname Spider, came into the kitchen to grab an apple from the refrigerator.

"Are you going to make me leave if I don't get a job?"

"I'm looking every day for a job for you." Jay rubbed his eyes. "To be honest, after Christmas it's going to be that much harder to find something. But we will. I keep praying for it. God's got a plan for you."

He realized abruptly that Eddie, Spider and Louis were all staring at him. His mind raced back along his last words to figure out what had piqued their interest.

Spider was the one to throw the lifeline. "God's got a plan for us?"

"Definitely." Spider had ghosted around the rectory and the Caf since the summertime. "God has a plan for every person He made."

Eddie said, "What's my plan?"

Jay chuckled. "That's the thing—we don't know what the plan is at first. We have to grow into it."

"Could you ask God for me?"

Jay chuckled. "I'm not sure God would tell me that."

With a huff and an eye-roll, Spider shook his head. "God wouldn't want to talk to me."

"Maybe he does." Jay glanced at Kevin. "You make it hard to hear anything at all with the radios pounding away up there."

Kevin smirked. "Do you realize you just quoted Dad?"

Jay started. "Good grief. You're right."

Kevin turned aside, but not in time to hide the laugh.

Eddie said, "What does God sound like?"

Jay worked to look serious again. "It's not really a sound. It's more like you know it in your heart."

Eddie's face fell. "I don't know all that much."

"You don't need to know things out of books for God to speak to you." Jay smiled at Eddie. "God loves us the way we are, and he talks to us so that we can understand."

"My mom spoke Spanish sometimes," Louis said.

"Do you understand Spanish?" Jay said.

Louis said, "A little."

"Well, sometimes it's like that with God. You feel like it's a foreign language, but over time, you figure it out."

Spider tapped a rhythm on the table with a spoon. "But seriously, what kind of plan does God have for a bunch of kids? I can't go out there and fight crime or make world peace or any of that garbage."

"I have it on good authority that crime fighters and peace makers started out as kids too." Jay gave Spider a knowing smile, which Spider returned with another eye roll. "Right now, you can be there for each other." Jay looked over at the three little ones, who had left homes where they were separated in order to freeze together in a bus station. "You can stand up for each other as if you were defending God Himself."

~

Jay retrieved his blanket from one of the boys' rooms, replacing it with one of the sleeping bags Kevin had brought. He folded it, and they made their way downstairs.

"You've never been in the rectory before, have you?"

"Not other than the foyer." Kevin paused. "Should I have purified myself before entering?"

Jay huffed, pointing toward rooms on the ground floor. "Library. Conference room. Office. You'll notice the absence of a surgical suite."

In the basement apartment Kevin noted only a bathroom, a minuscule kitchen, the bedroom, and an unfinished boiler room with a washing machine. The entire basement had the same worn vinyl flooring, the walls a dingy yellow with a uniform drabness that meant it had been intentionally painted that way, although a decade previously. Maybe even two.

Where he'd expected to see pictures of the Virgin Mary and stern-faced saints in monk's robes, Kevin saw walls bare except for one crucifix in each room. A ragged-edged corkboard hung on the wall where it had possibly remained for the last twenty years.

Looking around the bedroom, Kevin said, "I've ticketed bigger SUVs."

Jay spread the scratchy blanket on a twin bed while Kevin ran his fingers over cracks in the walls.

"And it could use a coat of paint."

"Paint is ten dollars a gallon. I'd need two cans. Twenty dollars is eighty pounds of rice." Jay shrugged. "No one comes down here but me."

"Not even a housekeeper?"

"Are you volunteering to pay for one?" Jay chuckled. "Actually, the diocese would. We scoured every regulation the diocese has looking for anything they'd pay for. I found out they'd give St. Gus thirty dollars a month as a housekeeping cost to clean the rectory. I put Mrs. D. down as the housekeeper, we got the extra thirty bucks. It goes straight into the cafeteria fund, and I still clean my own bathtub."

Kevin laughed. "And to think Mom used to yell at us that we didn't have a maid. Okay, so no housekeeper, but now I'm down here, and *I* see it. Doesn't it depress you to live this way?"

"I don't have good enough vision to pay attention to the shortcomings." Jay opened his hands. "I have a bed, a kitchen, and a bathroom. What more do I need?"

"Why have a crucifix over your bed if you can't see it?"

"Touché." Jay shook his head. "I know it's there."

Jay rubbed his eyes, then removed his contact lenses and replaced his glasses. For some reason the change brought Kevin up short—maybe it was the distortion of Jay's eyes. Kevin stepped further into the room. The touch of Kevin's fingers brought away a coating of desiccated cork.

Jay had tacked up notes carefully printed in wavering small capitals, but what drew Kevin's attention were the photographs. Jay and the other three priests ordained with him occupied the upper left hand corner. On the right hand side was a photograph of Jay with their parents. Some other photographs seemed to be groups from the church itself, the youth group, the choir, and other gatherings Kevin couldn't identify. There was one photograph of Kevin and Jay together, taken on Christmas morning when they were still boys. Jay was looking right at the camera lens; Kevin was looking at the lighted tree. It had been one of their mother's favorite photographs. She always pointed to Kevin's misdirected gaze and said, "Loot!" There was a similar photo taken that afternoon at the dinner table, now in a box in Kevin's closet. Jay had posed with an overstacked forkful of turkey and his mouth open wide enough to swallow an egg sideways. Their mother would point to that one next and say, "Food!"

A sudden burst of squabbling voices came from upstairs, followed by first one booming radio, then a second.

"That kid Nick," Kevin said. "He's trouble."

"You're telling me?"

"Why do you let him stay?"

Jay opened his hands and raised his eyebrows.

Kevin huffed. "Oh. You think you're going to convert him?"

"I'm not trying to convert any of them. You can't preach to an empty stomach. These kids have so many immediate needs right now that there's no way they could listen to preaching."

Kevin frowned. "Then why are you doing it?"

"It's called compassion."

"That kid Nick isn't all that compassionate."

"Spider was angrier than Nick, if you can believe it." Jay looked up. "It took about three weeks, but when he realized I wasn't about to boot him out, he relaxed." Jay moved toward the chair in the corner and settled himself in as it creaked. He sighed while staring at the window. "I knew Spider was on the mend when he offered to fix the hole he punched in the wall."

"I don't like this." Kevin folded his arms and leaned against the doorframe. "Any one of those boys could kill you while you sleep."

"Hey," Jay said with a grin. "Martyrdom."

"Hey," Kevin replied without the grin. "Dead."

"Dead is under-rated. God's waiting for us on the other side. Yeah, yeah, don't get all defensive on me. I believe God is waiting for me on the other side and that it's worth the price of passage. You don't. I know."

Kevin shrugged.

"Nick will come around." Jay cocked his head. "Or he won't. It's not up to me. As for preaching, eventually every one of them says what you do—why is he doing this for us? At that point, they'd have to be blind not to see the answer is that I'm doing it because of God. That will make them question a little more about who God is and what God does. If God makes good things come their way, they're going to be a little more receptive to who God is. If only because they think they'll get more good stuff by tolerating my little idiosyncrasies." Jay shrugged. "For them, it's practical."

"If you believe any of it."

Jay shrugged. "Right. That's if you believe any of it. If you don't believe it, then I'm doing it for a lie, but at least they're getting a place to sleep and something to eat."

He slowly pulled himself up from his chair. "When do you have to get going?"

"My tour begins at two."

"Then come help out your lying brother. I have to get things set up at the Caf."

In the church basement was a hall the size of an auditorium filled with lunchroom tables. Jay called, "Mrs. D?"

A woman in her early sixties wearing a canvas apron poked her head from a small room off to the side. "Father Jay—"

Jay jerked a thumb at Kevin. The woman's eyes widened, and she beamed at Jay. "Oh, thank heaven—come on, we're running late already!"

"You see," Jay said as he ushered Kevin into a long hot room lined with two menthol-green refrigerators, a sink, a grill and a stove dating from World War II, "we were praying for you to come, even though we didn't know at the time it was you."

With a smile that dimpled her round face, Mrs. D. handed Kevin a five-pound bag of carrots and a peeler.

Kevin said, "Does the Church support slavery?"

"Not slavery—volunteering!"

Kevin opened the bag. "It's not volunteering. I've been volun*told*."

Jay touched Kevin on the shoulder as he squeezed through in the narrow space between work table and countertop. "We serve lunch in about an hour, and it's a four-person job, three-person minimum. Two people bailed on us yesterday afternoon, I guess because they're busy this close to the holidays, leaving me and Mrs. D. to run the show ourselves for the rest of the week." He began washing tomatoes in a metal sink large enough to bathe a Golden Retriever. "You're welcome to eat with us afterward. Thursday's rice and beans day."

Mrs. D. was the powerhouse who answered the phones for the parish, typed the bulletin, and helped run the St. Gus soup kitchen. Priests tended to stay in one spot for five years; Mrs. D. had been a fixture through the last three priests and knew its workings better than Jay. "It's going to be tight today," Mrs. D. said. "We have enough rice, but we're practically out of beans."

"God will provide." All the same, the soup kitchen got more clients during the holiday season and fewer donations. Upscale parishes donated turkey dinners to needy families, but here in the poorest part of the city, sometimes the best they could do was rice and beans, or spaghetti.

She sighed as she unloaded bags of rolls onto the stainless steel counter. "I wish God would tell us how he was planning on providing it."

Kevin shot a look at Jay, but Jay only continued rinsing tomatoes, saying, "The same way he always does, I guess. He'll open someone's heart or else He'll remove the need."

"Wouldn't that be terrific?" Kevin kept his voice flat. "No more hunger in the world—just on account of one parish's prayers."

"How many parishes would have to pray, do you think?" Jay opened another bag of tomatoes. Suddenly he laughed. "Kevin, remember the story of that guy who says he has no idea that one cookie could cause such bad indigestion? Then he looks at ten empty boxes and says, 'I wonder which one it was.'"

Mrs. D. rubbed her hands on her jeans, then reached for a pair of latex gloves. "Jesus did say there'd always be poverty."

"He didn't add, 'So don't do anything about it.'" Jay moved over to the counter and sliced tomatoes in long even strokes. "I've heard in other countries even the poorest populations don't suffer a homelessness problem. They pull together."

Jay didn't add anything further as he made up the rest of the salad. Two tremendous bowls were necessary to feed the forty people who would come to the soup kitchen's lunch rush. It was never much of a meal—always a salad and a main dish of rice and beans, spaghetti with sauce, or some other cheap staple. Today they'd have rolls as well.

Kevin found himself caught up in the preparations. When the first people arrived, Jay left the kitchen and collared four of the young men. He showed Kevin how much rice and beans to put on each of the plates, and then he finished off each meal with a helping of salad and a thick slice of Italian bread. The four "waiters" took the full plates from the kitchen along with cups of orange or apple juice.

During a pause, Kevin said, "Why don't they just come to us?"

"Too much stigma, like a school lunchroom." Jay worked without sparing a moment to look at Kevin. "The younger ones like playing waiter, and that keeps everyone's dignity intact. It's important."

They said nothing else to one another during the initial lunch crush, and when the flow of people ended, Jay fixed plates for Kevin and himself. They made their way into the lunchroom where more than forty men, women and children were having their meals.

Before they found a pair of seats, Maria came flying up to Jay, screeching, with Louis at her heels.

"Woah!" He lifted his tray away from the pair as Maria ducked behind his legs, smacked Louis's arm, and then took cover again at his back. "What's going on?"

"He took my roll!" Maria shouted. "I had a bigger roll and when I opened my milk I turned and his roll was bigger than mine! He switched my roll and he said it was his and he took a bite out of it and now I don't have a big roll!"

"That was mine!" Louis was shouting at the same time. "I can't help it if you got a stinky roll! You can't take mine!"

Jay stuck his tray on the closest table and called the kids to order, which of course they refused to do.

When Maria jumped Louis again and started scratching, Kevin left his tray and separated the pair, pulling Louis off Maria.

"Leave me alone!" Louis was shouting.

"Get your hands off of him!" Maria hollered. "Leave my brother alone!"

Kevin released Louis, who shot him a filthy look.

On hearing the noise, Mrs. D. bore down on the kids. "Can the two of you talk without hurting one another? I can't understand either of you."

With many interruptions, the pair repeated their story: each laid claim to the better roll.

Mrs. D. said, "Let's take a look at these rolls."

Kevin watched in astonishment as the children led her to their plates and demonstrated for her the inadequacies of the one roll and the perfection of the other.

Mrs. D. agreed with the children's assessment, and then, to Kevin's surprise, she cut both rolls in half, giving each child half of the good roll and half of the disliked roll (with Louis getting the bitten part).

Both kids gazed up at her in awe.

Jay murmured, "And I thought Solomon did good with the baby thing."

Kevin didn't ask for clarification. Looking around the room, he saw the third child, the little one, was sitting on the lap of one of the bigger boys—the one who had opened the door last night.

Her work here finished, Mrs. D. returned to the kitchen, and Maria and Louis turned their attention to their meal.

Jay took a moment to lower himself into a chair at the table, then waited for Kevin to take a seat as well. "We have this kind of lunch every day." Jay looked shrunken as he rubbed his temples. "Holly helped us set it up. If it weren't for St. Gus, many of these folks wouldn't have a solid meal some days. Half this parish is under the poverty level, and the rest aren't much better off because their jobs only keep them from qualifying for government help." He closed his eyes for a long moment.

Assuming Jay was saying grace or blessing the food, Kevin waited until Jay looked up before he spoke again. "Who'd you annoy in the diocese to get sent to the worst parish in the world?"

"Should I make a list of people I've annoyed?" Jay offered a smile. "This neighborhood got hit hard when the economy tanked."

Kevin looked at the crowd. "You don't ever charge for the meal?"

Jay shook his head. "How can we? It doesn't matter if they come here on Sundays, even. Maybe a couple of folks are taking advantage of us, but the majority need the help. And it ensures that I get time for one meal a day too."

A lanky boy with a shock of blond hair and a red armband came up behind Jay and took the seat beside him. "Hey, Farrell—who's this?"

Jay said, "Masa, aren't you supposed to be in school?"

"Half day, remember? Christmas break." The boy turned his large smile to Kevin. "You know he used to be a soldier?"

Kevin took a drink of water. "You don't say?"

Masa nodded eagerly. "I keep hoping he'll teach me to shoot a gun for real, like they do in a war." A kid his age should have been playing air guitar with the radio, but Masa took a moment to play "air rifle" for Kevin, then turned to Jay. "You're gonna get me into West Point someday, right?"

"I'd rather see that enthusiasm on CYO basketball." Jay tousled the kid's hair. "I can't get you into West Point, but I can write you a letter of recommendation to the seminary in ten years."

"Yeah, yeah...but they could use me too!" The kid jumped off his seat and with a flourish drew a six-inch knife from his belt.

Kevin's eyes widened.

Jay's voice dropped half an octave. "You know you're not supposed to bring that in here."

"I know, but Freddie and Brad brought theirs yesterday, and—"

Jay wore the expression that had been able to scare Iraqi soldiers when he'd carried no other weapon. "And this is still a church. Even Saint Michael the Archangel would have to sheathe his sword in my church, got it? We're going to have another talk about this at Monday's youth group."

Masa stepped backward. "Hey, don't we do a good job for you?"

Jay looked at Kevin. "Masahiro's a member of the Archangels."

"They're *my* gang." Masa puffed up a little. "There hasn't been a single break-in or any graffiti since we started. We go with Farrell every night to

Frederick's to get the extra bread, and no one hassles him."

Jay looked amused. "So far they listen to me and there hasn't been any bloodshed."

Masa said, "I'd have gotten that one guy—"

"—except that you know who you have to go to for Confession." Jay gave the kid a blood-chilling smile. "How does reading all four Gospels sound for penance?"

Masa said, "You killed people."

"The army is a lot different from a gang. I've explained that before." Jay put out a hand. "Turn over the knife. I'm not kidding."

Masa thrust it to him hilt-first. Jay set it on the table alongside the plastic fork, and Masa stalked away with his shoulders hunched. Jay watched the boy retreat for a moment before calling across the hall, "Remember you're serving Christmas morning at nine!"

Kevin leaned forward. "I wouldn't be out of bounds to arrest him for possession of a deadly weapon."

Jay traced a finger along the flat of the blade. "Well, now you've got to arrest me instead. The kid has a heart the size of the parking lot, but he gets too enthusiastic."

"I can't believe you tell them about the war."

"I have to tell them about the war, Kevin. I can't pull a homily out of my hat. What I say has to come out of my life."

"So you tell a thousand total strangers about the war, and you never even spoke to me about the war?"

Silence: served up long and cold.

Jay finally said, "Have you ever had a call where you just never want to think about it again? Something you would rather die than tell to someone who really knows you?"

For a heartbeat, Kevin could see a porch with white Christmas lights, could see a car flipped on its roof.

Jay looked down. "In some senses my parishioners are entrusting me with their souls. They don't know me like you do. Telling them was a credibility issue."

Kevin shook off images of broken glass and a numb-eyed mother. "It doesn't impeach your credibility with them that ten years ago you were knee-deep in blood?"

"No more than it impeaches St. Paul's credibility that he helped stone St. Stephen." Jay tried to look sidelong at his brother. "At least they can accept that I've changed."

"Yeah, you've certainly changed." Kevin shoved aside his empty styrofoam plate. "I remember when *you* would have been the kid bringing the knife into the church."

"Would you rather I spent the rest of my life in jail?"

"That's not what I would have rather had at all, and you know it."

Jay opened his hands. "You don't get it both ways. The thing that saved my conscience was the same thing that saved my soul."

Kevin shook his head.

"Please, don't start this again," Jay said. "You know I can't stand it."

"I've told you I accept you the way that you are."

"You say that as though I have a disease." Jay looked at his lap. "I love you from the bottom of my heart, and I pray for you every day. I want nothing but good for you—and in return, you'll *tolerate* me. Like I'm an aged flatulent uncle you visit once a week for the sake of your long-dead grandmother."

Kevin stalked from the table and dropped his empty styrofoam plate into the trash, then got some more water. The makeshift cafeteria was emptying. It was one-thirty, and he'd have to leave in fifteen minutes for his shift. A volunteer dragged a dented metal trashcan from table to table and clearing the debris. By the time Kevin returned to his place, his pulse had calmed to something near normal and his hands had unclenched. Jay covered his face in his palms.

Kevin said, "You're wasting your life."

"How dare you—" Jay's voice broke. He struggled before continuing. "What are you saying—that you'd rather have had me in Hell ten years ago?"

Kevin snorted. "Hell, hell, hell. You knew you were going to hell back then—how many times did you say that to other people: *I'll see you in Hell*?"

Jay looked pale. "I didn't have any idea back then. I honestly didn't care. My whole life was a little hell of its own, and I didn't know any better because—"

"—because you were fighting a *war*—"

"I'm still fighting a war!"   All motion silenced in the kitchen as Jay's voice rose in volume. "I feed forty people a day! I know you think everything I believe is wrong, but I found someplace I'm necessary, someplace I'm fulfilled! Why can't you accept that?"

Kevin folded his arms. "You ran away."

"I nearly died!"   Jay got to his feet and started cramming empty plates and cups and forks into a trash can. "Haven't I given enough? I lost my career, my vision, my balance, and my brother—isn't that enough to justify listening to what's going on inside?"

Jay grabbed Masa's confiscated knife and hurled it into the can with a clamorous bang.

Kevin folded his arms and straightened. "You're right about one thing because you have given up everything.   And for what? I don't see any God waltzing through your life restoring your sight or your balance or giving you back anything for what you threw away in the first place."

Jay's eyes glimmered ferociously. "God won't be outdone in generosity."

Kevin choked on a laugh and looked off at one of the cafeteria walls. "I'll say.   When it comes to payback, God stops at 'nothing'."

Jay's glare bored into him with a soul-stopping intensity, but after all these years, it was a serve Kevin could return.

Jay looked away, breathing hard, and resumed clearing the table. Kevin reached toward the table, and Jay imposed himself between Kevin and the trash can. "Don't touch anything. I don't need your help, if that's what you think you're doing. Believe it or not, I'm not dead, and I'm not an invalid, and I'm not insane."

Kevin took half a step back.

Jay's voice came unnaturally low. "Everyone here is going to Heaven or Hell, and I'm watching at the fulcrum. And you're telling me I'm running away? That I might as well be dead?"

Kevin caught his breath.

Jay said, "God gave me a second chance. Are you jealous?"

"I can't be jealous of a fraud." Kevin's eyes narrowed. "No one bent double by tragedy can ever stand up again. There are no second chances."

Jay kept his back to Kevin, and he leaned on the metal can with both hands. "This is the truth, Kevin—I miss you so much it hurts. But if that's what you think of me, I'd prefer if you never came back again."

Kevin's jaw locked. Jay looked at the can half full of trash, let out a deep breath, then walked past Kevin. He pushed open the squeaky door to the fluorescent light of the kitchen.

Good job, Kevin. He thrust his hands into his pockets and avoided looking toward the volunteers as he walked up the stairs and exited to the parking lot.

Six

Sometimes Kevin knew beyond all doubt that Jay had been saved by God, his life if not his soul. Flying to be with Jay at the German hospital, Kevin had even tried to pray because he remembered praying for their mother: *God, if you exist, please keep him alive. Please give him back to me.*

It hadn't worked to save his mother, but the second time around, it had. Something had. Maybe God only batted .500.

But for several months it looked as though Kevin's prayer had served only to keep Jay trapped in a useless body, a souvenir of a life once lived, preserved to be gawked at and have its IV bags changed every six hours.

What kind of life have I prayed up for you? Kevin wondered, trying to hope that if God did exist, that maybe God had ignored his ill-advised prayer and done whatever had been in the plan to begin with.

In those early days, someone stayed at Jay's bedside while they waited for the end, and all that night Jay slept with a morphine-induced calm that misrepresented his whole life. Nearly three weeks later, Dad was the one in the room when Jay first opened his eyes. Straightening, Dad called his name, but Jay only fumbled at his face with one clumsy hand, trying to remove a nonexistent blindfold. Before Dad finished paging the nurses, Jay submerged into sleep again. Within an hour he roused a second time, this time with Kevin nearby.

Jay awakened totally blind. Dad explained as simply as he could whatever he thought Jay wanted to know while Kevin held Jay's hand. Jay hadn't stayed conscious long, but he indicated he wasn't in pain. He tugged once at the tube of the ventilator before lying limp again.

Seeing Jay in bed like a corpse had been awful, and having to stand in the room watching Jay slip back into semi-consciousness worse still. But of all those weeks, the moment most wrenching for Kevin happened seven days after Jay had risen from the coma. While he sat alongside Jay's bed speaking awkwardly about something unimportant, Jay had signed to him, *Take it off.*

Kevin said, "Take what off?"

Jay pointed to the respirator tube.

Kevin's hands went utterly cold. "I can't—it'll kill you."

Jay signed again, *Take it off.*

His hands trembled so badly Kevin found it hard to make out the signs they'd used when coordinating mayhem out on the streets.

Jay tugged again at the tube in his throat. So many inconveniences—Kevin had never needed a respirator, but he knew how someone's lips could get chapped from the constant suction of the air. Jay had been on it a week. It stopped him from talking or eating, and it trapped him in the bed. "Can't you bear it a little longer?" Kevin said. His hands now shook worse than Jay's. "You can't breathe without it. It's got to stay on." Machines did everything for Jay's body at that time.

Jay pointed again to the tube and tugged at it. He raised a hand to sign once more, then dropped it back to the blankets.

Kevin pushed the button for the nurse, and when she arrived, he asked her to shut off the ventilator.

"Not without his doctor present," the nurse said.

Kevin said, "Then get his doctor. Now. He has the right to refuse treatment, and I'll shut it off myself."

Jay swiveled grateful eyes in the direction of Kevin's voice.

Dad arrived with a doctor, and the doctor ordered the nurse to give Jay a sedative. Jay refused. Dad snapped, "If they're pulling that tube out, you need to be knocked out. Stop messing around." Jay didn't argue any longer. He didn't have a choice, Kevin realized. All these machines kept him trapped in this world, and he couldn't move his body enough to disengage any of them. For the moment, Kevin was his voice and Kevin was his hands.

As Jay drifted to sleep, Dad gestured that Kevin leave the room. Kevin shook his head. Dad said, "I'm not going to fight with you in here. Follow me."

Next door, Dad and two of Jay's medical team plus the hospital chaplain and one of the ethicists held a meeting with the four remaining team members. One doctor refused to turn off the machine. One pointed out that if it was stressing Jay, its removal might speed his recovery. Both doctors admitted Jay would probably breathe on his own for a while, but in the long term he might not be able to keep up the work.

Kevin was concerned turning off the machine would be murder, but the round-faced, grey-haired chaplain assured him that a respirator was an extraordinary treatment. Dad was of the opinion that if Jay could breathe on his own, the machine should stay off, but if he went into respiratory distress he should be intubated again.

Such a queer discussion, so insulated. Kevin couldn't believe how clinically everyone discussed ending his brother's life.

When they came around to Kevin, he repeated what he'd said before: although he hated it, Jay had the right to refuse treatment. Jay was competent to make the decision.

They returned to Jay's room. Jay slept gently, but Kevin felt the green horror of the numbers on the monitor branding itself into his mind. In these last minutes, this might be all he had left of Jay, just a bunch of stupid numbers. 47, 8, 62, 95/50.

Jay's body gagged as they removed the tube, and Kevin stood cold in the corner with Dad until the medics finished. A new nurse guided another breathing apparatus over Jay's mouth and fastened it with straps behind his ears, then slipped his hair free of the elastic with a tender hand. This jetted oxygen up to him but didn't force it into his lungs, and because it was less invasive, Jay would be able to talk again. The doctors also removed the feeding tube, but they left the glucose solution IV intact. Finally a nurse raised the head of the bed. Throughout, Jay had kept breathing steadily, inching up every time he drew breath.

Kevin approached Jay in the darkened room, glanced at the monitor, and then sat at the bedside.

Dad said, "He's doing all right for now."

Kevin whispered, "I'm scared." The admission surprised him. In the dusk of the room, he felt death so much nearer than with a machine to keep it at bay.

Dad took a deep breath, but before saying anything he walked out of the room.

Kevin said lowly, "Jay? I made them take it off. I'm sorry. I know it's what you want, but I'm still sorry. I made them do it."

As if rousing from a dream, Jay fluttered open his eyes. He extended a hand, and Kevin caught it by reflex after so many times this week. Jay raised his other hand to his mouth, then pursed his lips, swallowed, and sighed.

He rasped the words, "Thank you."

Kevin put his head on the bed against Jay's side and cried. But Jay kept breathing, and when morning came, it found him breathing still.

Seven

Good job, Jay.

Yep, that's why he'd gone to seminary and gotten ordained: in order to yell at his brother. Wonderful that he could preach about loving your enemy and then lose his temper with Kevin.

Jay wished for once that he could still head to a gym to pummel a sandbag and then run on a treadmill until he outdistanced himself. Instead he sat at a table in the upstairs kitchen, pounded out a Christmas homily, and ignored the telephone when it rang in the parish office. Let Mrs. D. take the calls. She could handle anything, and if he was needed, she knew where he was.

Yes, yet another thing he could ask forgiveness for. Why was he able to listen to the most outrageous things in the confessional without even remembering them afterward, but his brother instantly sent him into a rage?

Your brother could always push your buttons. Why? Because Jay and Kevin had helped install one another's buttons. It only made sense.

Jay looked at the crucifix and said, "See, you're lucky. You didn't have a younger brother."

Footsteps above Jay caught his attention. He often heard footsteps in the basement, but here he was at the top floor. Meaning the only place above him was the roof.

After a moment, he heard them again, along with some of the boys calling to one another. He went to the window and focused as hard as he could. Three dark shapes moved about beneath the window, which he slid up to stick his head outside.

"Hey, Father Jay!"

That didn't come from the ground, nor from directly overhead. Jay looked straight out at the telephone pole at the curb. "Spider? What are you doing?"

"We're gonna have cable, Father! There's a ton of Christmas specials on this week."

Oh, for the love of little green apples. His breath frothed out in the frigid air, and he felt the heat getting sucked from the building. Jay said, "You can't do that."

Spider sounded cheerful. "Sure I can. My dad taught me how."

"Terrific. My dad taught me how to change a tire."

"My dad did that too."

"Spider, get down from there."

Everyone stopped moving. From above, Nick said, "Why?"

"I'm not having you guys steal cable."

"I bought the cable from my job at the hardware store. They even gave me the employee discount."

Jay counted to three in his head. "You know what I'm talking about."

"How can it be stealing? It's not like everyone else isn't going to have it because of this."

"Theft of services. No."

"I'm not stealing anyone's service either. I'm doing it myself."

Jay knew it was wrong; in the heat of the moment he couldn't figure out exactly why. "I'm not debating moral theology while you're twenty feet in the air. Just get the heck down from there and get inside. All of you."

"Aw, Father!"

Jay pulled his head into the kitchen and slammed the window. He waited, braced for impact. Footsteps scrambled over on the roof until they reached the fire-escape, and one of the bedroom windows slid up with a wooden hiss. Downstairs, the front door opened, and a large number of feet trooped up the stairs. Shortly five boys (well, four boys and Maria) assembled in the kitchen.

Jay knew better than to expect a warm-up from Nick. "What the hell is your problem?" Nick shouted. "Well? Nobody gives a shit if we're running a line from the street into the house!"

"I care."

"Nobody but you, then!" Jay could feel Nick's breath, the boy was so close. "Are you afraid we're all going to hell because we watch a few TV programs without paying a boatload of money to some fat cows in big offices who don't even care if we—"

"Nick, calm down."

"I don't have to calm down! What the hell could anyone possibly care about whether we watch TV or not?"

Jay folded his arms. "I'm not having this discussion with you screaming."

"Hey, chill." Spider pushed Nick back a step. "Get a grip."

"What kind of stupid—"

"Sit down, man." Spider thrust Nick toward one of the chairs. "I'm serious. Sit. You're making an idiot out of yourself."

"Who does he think he is?"

"He owns the house." Spider upticked his voice so it sounded more like a question than a statement. *"That's* who he is. And unless they have cable piped into the cardboard boxes behind McDonalds, you better remember that."

Nick pulled out the chair. "Fine. You go kissing his ass."

Eddie came into the kitchen in response to all the noise. Jay said, "I'll talk to you about it in a minute, Nick. But first, Spider, you know I can't have you running an illegal cable line into the rectory."

Spider pointed to Jamie and Maria. "It's for the kids. They want to watch the Christmas specials."

"That's extraordinarily generous of you, willing to go to jail for the kids."

"No one's going to jail over this, man. You just run the line in and hook it up, and no one cares."

Spider slipped his hands in his pockets. "The cable guys don't even care. Geez, it was a cable guy who showed us how to do it in the first place."

Jay folded his arms and regarded Spider.

"You're not going to let us do it?"

Jay raised one eyebrow.

"You suck," Nick said.

"It's the law." Jay sighed. "Maybe it doesn't make sense, but stealing is stealing, and you are bunking in a Catholic church for now."

Spider said, "What about the kids?"

"What about them? When did TV become a daily requirement?"

An uncomfortable silence filled the kitchen until Eddie said, "But it's Christmas shows. Like Rudolph the Red Nosed Reindeer."

"And that movie about Santa Claus coming to Macy's."

"And that other one about the angel getting its wings when the bells ring."

Jay's heart caught, and he averted his gaze.

What could be more normal than sitting in front of the TV at Christmas watching those silly Rankin and Bass shows? Or any movie with Santa Claus? No, it wasn't a mandatory requirement. But hadn't they already lost so much just by being homeless and not having families who cared whether they died?

"Are you going to let us?" said Spider.

"I'll think of something," Jay said, "but you can't hook up stolen cable TV."

"I hate you," Nick said.

"Maybe you've never heard of the invention of the VCR," Jay said, "or the DVD player. I have. Someone can loan us the shows, and you can have your TV the right way." He looked at Spider and thought he could make out the boy's grin. "Not only will you not be stealing, but then someone else gets to be generous."

Nick stalked away, and the other kids dispersed. The boys' music went on at concentration-shattering volumes, so Jay gathered his books to head back downstairs. He caught motion from his peripheral vision. "Eddie? Could you help me carry these?"

As they descended into the basement, the air turned sweltering. Last winter, before he'd heated the upstairs, he'd depended on an unreliable space heater to get at least his bedroom warm (offering prayers every day that it not burn down the rectory). The heat had never penetrated the bathroom or the kitchen. This year, heating the upstairs, he was tempted to open a window or take off his shirt. When he'd first moved in, he'd wondered about those pipes running across the basement ceiling. He'd hung is clothes on them to dry. Now he knew. The pipes carried steam upstairs but seemed to shed all the actual heat right over his head.

"You can just put those all on the desk."

Eddie shuffled into the room and put down the stack. "Father Jay? Can I ask a question?"

Jay asked him to sit, and the boy did. Sometimes Jay wished he had better vision, because even with glasses he couldn't make out Eddie's face clearly. He suspected Eddie looked different since the storeowners often rejected him on sight. No, they couldn't use a boy to do work for them. No, they wouldn't make a job for him. No, no, no. It was worse than giving away kittens, and once Jay had gotten stuck doing that too.

"They said I'm lazy. Because I don't have a job."

Jay swallowed. "I've been looking for one. It's hard to find one now."

"Nick came after I did." Eddie thought a moment. "Nick has a job."

Nick very nearly didn't have a job, not after he'd had a shouting match with a patron at the Italian restaurant. Jay almost ransomed his soul to keep Nick employed.

Eddie's shoulder slumped. "It's because I'm stupid."

"You're not stupid." That much came automatically, but after that Jay groped for the words. "It's hard to find the right fit for you. Nick would fit in anywhere if he worked at it. I know you'll work hard wherever you end up. You're a good kid. But it's hard to find the right place for you."

Eddie processed it all. "You think I'm a good kid?"

"When I need help, you're the first by my side. You're generous and giving. And you're sensitive, which is why you take it to heart when the boys tease you."

A small blond presence at the door interrupted Jay.

Eddie had a large grin. "Jamie!"

He scooped the little boy in his arms, and with a grin he cuddled the boy against his chest. "I was coming up soon."

Jamie clung to Eddie's shoulders and pushed his face into his neck. Eddie exchanged a smile with Jay. "I'll take him up."

Jay nodded. "You get along well with them."

Eddie left, but then turned back at the door. "Thanks."

Jay chuckled, and then he was alone again with his almost-written homily.

Why did Nick have to harass Eddie like that? Weren't all the boys in the same boat? Why find the one most vulnerable and try to drive him away? There wasn't much upstairs, but there was shelter and food enough to go around.

Thinking of Nick and the boy's open antagonism, Jay grew cold even in the sweltering basement. He wasn't joking with Kevin—Spider had been just as bad when he'd arrived in the summer, hot and hungry, hanging out on the fringes of the Archangels, eating one meal a day from the Caf and vanishing in-between times, until the winter had driven him into the upstairs like an animal sensing shelter.

Jay had no clue what had reached Spider, no clue what would reach Nick.

Last summer, Jay had borrowed a bunch of garden tools from a suburban parish and tilled up a little parish garden, the idea being that he would plant tomatoes and use them for the Caf. It had been a fun project: he called it Seed Time and explained one week during his homily that sixty-nine cents worth of seeds yields about a hundred dollars worth of tomatoes, and that something was going to grow on the parish lawn, so they might as well eat it. Brandishing a copy of Mrs. D's recipe for Dandelion Soup, he'd threatened everyone with it unless they showed up to help plow the ground and set the garden.

Afterward, weeding the cleared plot was Jay's responsibility. The dirt, while apparently not well-suited to tomatoes, was Heaven itself as far as the dandelions and the thistles were concerned. Mrs. D. warned him that no one had ever won a war against thistles, but Jay did. Every day he went out in the mid-morning after Mass and, using the time to meditate, scanned the ground with his pinpoint vision, uprooting any little shoots one at a time. Over the course of the entire summer, eventually he would wear them out so the leftover roots would expend all their energy and die underground.

One mid-morning with the temperatures set to top ninety-five, Spider had wandered over from the alley behind the nearest tenement. The only other motion was the priest weeding the garden.

Jay noticed as Spider's shadow fell across the vegetable garden. The words appeared in his head: *Whoever receives a small child such as this has received me.*

Okay, he thought to God. *Bring it on.*

Then he chuckled. "It's kind of hot this morning."

Spider just sat, knees hugged to his chest.

Jay pulled up another dandelion. "What brings you out here?"

Spider shrugged. "So, you want me to get some tools?"

Jay usually just got his hands into the soil, but he said, "That would be good."

Spider walked away. He'd been hanging around the church for three weeks at this point.

When he'd returned, dumping a few trowels and a weeding tool onto the soil, Spider squatted, watching Father Jay work, then took a trowel and started unearthing thistles. Jay said, "Make sure you get the root, otherwise it'll have to be weeded again."

"Huh?"

"Thistles have tap roots, big roots that go all the way down. If you just pull off the leaves, the thistle grows back."

Spider tugged too hard and broke the root. "How do you do that?"

"You'll get a feel for it. Try a more gentle pull and twist, and see if you can get your fingers around the root."

They worked in silence. As the sun grew higher, Jay said something about sunburn, but there are things that hurt worse than sunburn, so together they persevered. After a quarter of the bed was clear, Spider's slightly accented voice said, "So, you talk a lot with God, right?"

Jay sat back. "I do."

"So did he ever tell you why there's all this evil shit in the world?"

Jay dusted his hands on his pants. "No, he never explained about that."

Spider's hardened face was like a mask. "But really. I mean, why does God let awful things happen?"

"There's theory, and there's your life. I could give you a lecture about free will, but your eyes would glaze over and you'd walk away convinced I didn't care. A lecture could never answer your real question, which is 'Why me? Why my life?'"

Spider kept working. "My stepdad threw me out of the house. He said he'd kill me if I went back. My mom said I'd better go. I'm just waiting for the whiskey to finish him off."

Jay groped for the right words to tell the kid his mother actually did love him, and he found his mind blank, so he said nothing. The Bible said the Holy Spirit would tell the disciples what to say; Jay himself always figured that was as good a cue as any that the Holy Spirit wanted him to shut up.

Spider said, "So I can't go home again until the guy kicks off. What am I going to do?"

Jay murmured, "What are you going to do?" The sun had gotten still higher, and they'd lost any shade from the nearby trees. Even the cars passing on the street sounded hot, their engines muffled by the humidity as if the noise was too exhausted to carry far. "You'll be a survivor. You'll plug away automatically for a while, and one day it'll come right down to it and you'll have to decide what you want. It may take years. You'll feel like you survived for a reason, and you'll have to figure out what that reason is. You will never get over it, but you'll carry it forward with you. Your mom's choice, your stepdad's boozing—all that will never be good, but you'll have made good come out of it. It'll probably grow so deep down inside you that eventually you can't imagine yourself without it."

Spider's voice remained flat. "I hate them both."

"I don't blame you."

"How messed up do you have to be to kick out your own kid?"

Jay said, "Do you hate God?"

Spider looked up in fear.

"I think it's understandable," and Jay made sure to keep his tone calm, "to be so mad you can't even speak to God for a long time. But you've got to do something with the rage, if only to keep it from burning yourself out."

"So you think I should go to church and talk to God?"

"I think you should do whatever helps," Jay said. "Even if it's weeding a flower bed."

Spider turned his head aside. "Well, I'm not becoming a priest." When Jay laughed out loud, Spider said, "I'd rather be a soldier like you were. Or a cop."

"The police and I are doing the same work." Jay sat back on his heels, rubbing the dirt granules from his palms. "They're cutting off the leaves, and I'm pulling out the roots. What you're going to learn, Spider, is that evil has taproots. You can slice it apart all you want, but if that root's intact below, the leaves will show up again. You've never completely weeded a garden. But it helps to be doing something, and both kinds of work are worthwhile."

"I don't really get you. You became a priest to fight bad guys?"

"I became a priest because I fell headfirst into something I didn't understand but loved anyhow. Keeping up the fight is an unexpected bonus. It's like getting back something you thought you'd lost forever."

Spider said, "I want my home back."

Jay winced. "If I could, I'd give it to you."

Without another word, Spider arose and walked away.

In that summertime brightness, Jay had looked at his dirt-covered knees and thought, *There wasn't anything I could have said that would have helped him, but shouldn't I have been able to do better than that?*

But here it was, months later, and that had been the first moment of Spider's turn-around, a moment where God had succeeded when Jay thought his own efforts had failed.

Dear God, let it come down to that moment with Nick, where the weeding would be done and Jay could begin planting. Spider had turned around. Jay himself had turned around. God could turn Nick around too, given time. Given prayer. Given patience and love. And those were all gifts God had in abundance.

Eight

At midnight on December 23rd, the restaurant owner approached Holly and told her she could have their leftover bread for the Caf. She dialed Kevin's cell phone and reached him at work. "I was wondering if you could stop by and pick it up so Jay will have it in the morning."

"I don't think Jay wants to talk to me right now."

Holly paused. "Could you just leave it with someone else? I'm not sure if I'll have a chance to get there tomorrow."

Sounding reluctant, Kevin agreed.

The restaurant officially closed at midnight, but a group of six had been seated at eleven-thirty and was still finishing their meal. Holly had two tables remaining; the only other waitress on duty was Sara, with the party of six and no one else. Holly began cleaning up in preparation for closing.

At twelve-thirty, Kevin walked in the door, and Holly escorted him to the kitchen where Luis and Cassandra were putting together a box for St. Gus. There was the typical give-and-take between the restaurant owners and a police officer—here, have something on the house, no I can't, no please, I can't accept—

Sara rushed into the back with tears on her face. "Those creeps left me a religious tract for a tip!"

"They did what?"

"It looks like a twenty on the front, but it's an invitation to their church—"

Holly snatched it from Sara's hand and raced for the front of the restaurant. She heard the chair scrape behind her as Kevin got up.

His words hung in the air behind her: "Don't make me arrest you for assault."

Holly didn't pause to grab her coat. It was easy to find the group in the parking lot. They hadn't yet gotten into their car.

"Excuse me," she called, "but which of you is responsible for this?"

They all turned.

"A tract alone is not a tip." Holly handed it to the man preparing to get behind the steering wheel. "I don't know where you come from, but in my world, waitresses need to pay for milk and bread with real money at the grocery store."

The woman in the passenger seat stepped out of the car. "You cannot serve both God and money."

"*The worker is worth his hire.* You wouldn't be happy with me if I were to go to your church and drop our take-out menu in the collection basket." Holly folded her arms. It hadn't started to snow yet, but the cold was bitter. "Call it what you want, but what you did was theft of services. How you treat the poor man is how you treat Jesus himself. Your server stayed an hour late taking care of your party while her son is sleeping on her mother's couch. She has to tip out the busboys from your check whether you give her the money or not, so she actually lost money for the privilege of bringing you dessert and refilling your coffee."

The woman looked shocked.

The man said, "I don't like your tone, miss."

"I'm sorry if you don't like it. No one liked what Jesus had to say either because it was the truth." Holly turned away. "Don't just preach to the world and tell the poor to be warm and well-fed. Show some compassion—for God's sake."

The man shook his head. "You clearly don't know the Lord."

"I know the Lord quite well. I would never dream of tipping with only His Word." Holly rubbed her frozen arms. "You want to make an impact—leave a real twenty and your tract." She took a step away, then looked over her shoulder. "By the way, my name is Holly if you want to get me fired. The woman you stiffed was Sara."

Back inside, Holly found Kevin at the door. She couldn't read the look on his face as he said, "You okay?"

"I hate that." She rubbed her eyes. "I don't care if they're cheap, but don't glorify it by saying God wants it. Waitresses get this kind of garbage all the time—'Why would I tip fifteen percent when God only gets ten?' God doesn't have to pay the bills." She leaned against the wall and tucked her chin. "This stinks, Kevin. She should have had eighteen dollars at least off that table. They ordered drinks and dessert, the works."

Kevin shook his head. "Come on in back."

"I've got to check my tables. I'll be there in a bit."

Holly went to the last two tables, apologized if they had been waiting for her, and refilled their coffee.

"Excuse me," a voice said. "Miss?"

Holly turned and found the woman from the car. "If you don't mind—" The woman's eyes were already watery, and now the dam burst. "I— We were wrong." She wiped her mascara-stained cheeks. "Could you—"

She held out some money to Holly, and Holly reached out to embrace the woman. Holly felt her breath catch and her eyes burning. "I'm sorry. I shouldn't have—"

"You should have." The woman bit her lip. "You were right."

Sara came from the back, and Holly waved her over. The woman gave her the money and apologized again, and she hugged Sara before leaving.

"Oh my God," Sara whispered, "she gave me forty dollars!"

Holly laughed. "Real this time?"

"Real. Do you know—" Sara looked at her. "Now you're going to make me cry. I can get Justin something else for Christmas. I only bought that sweatshirt for him. He'd have been happy with it, but there was a train set at Odd Lot, and now I can get it for him."

Holly smiled. "Merry Christmas."

And then she caught sight of Kevin's astonished face as he watched her from near the coat rack.

"She came back?"

Holly beamed. "She did!"

"I wouldn't have believed it." Kevin blinked. "What do you think changed her mind?"

Holly laughed. "I think it must have been God."

Nine

*T*he morning of December 24th, Jay opened the front door to a sheet of glass.

Unbelievable. Yes, last night's weather reports had predicted freezing rain—but this defied description. As smooth as a hockey-rink, the front steps of the rectory were only the first obstacle Jay needed to pass in order to get into the church for the morning Mass. Even with all his balance and perfect eyesight, he'd have been nervous.

Behind him, Eddie said, "You okay, Father?"

"Can you see any cars in the parking lot?"

Eddie slowly counted to seven. Jay had been hoping for zero. He shut the front door while he found his crutches in the coat closet, then pulled the little teeth-ends over the rubber stoppers. He fit his wrists into the guides and gripped the handles.

Eddie said, "I'll take you."

Jay glanced sideways. Eddie sounded determined, so Jay let the boy help him down the three ice-coated front steps, then directly across the parking lot to the closest of the church entrances.

He would have broken his back if he'd tried this alone. Even Eddie had trouble making the walk, wearing rubber-soled sneakers. But with Eddie supporting him under one arm, Jay managed to get to the church and the relative safety of the carpet.

He thanked Eddie, who beamed with pride. With any luck, the boy would make it back without busting a leg.

After vesting up but before starting the service, Jay knelt in the chilly church in front of the tabernacle and tried to clear his mind. *Too much Christmas clutter,* he prayed. *It's hard to listen. It's hard to keep focus.*

Momentarily he felt a question: What is most important for the holiday? What does the Nativity mean? And then, *What do you want for Christmas?*

A dozen needs flooded Jay's mind: all of those boys upstairs who distrusted the world, the three little kids who'd rather be dead together than alive apart, Eddie and his yearning for a meaningful role in the world, and on the other extreme Holly who would all but pay Jay a stipend trying to take care of him. There was Kevin and all of his baggage, his anger and his brooding distances—and it was too much. There were so many more gaps. His parish needed so much. Fighting Iraqis hadn't sapped half as much out of him as St. Gus could on its busiest days.

Oh, God... Jay lowered his head to hide the nervous chuckle. *All I asked for was an electric can-opener.*

As Jay made his way back into the sacristy, he noticed those who entered through the side door had amused smiles. As he passed, one parishioner tapped twice on the holy water in the font: the water had frozen solid.

After morning Mass, someone came into the sacristy. "Father Farrell?"

He recognized the voice. "Hi, Mrs. D. Big day ahead."

"Wouldn't have it any other way. Listen, last night I was baking, and I ended up with too many cookies."

Sure. She had "ended up" making too many cookies in the same way she had "accidentally" bought too many turkeys at Thanksgiving and picked too many apples in October. "And I thought to myself that the boys upstairs might want some Christmas cookies. They might never have had any before in their lives. Would they like them?"

Jay accepted the weighty box—tied with a blue satin ribbon He assured her the cookies had no chance of surviving until Christmas morning.

The door opened, and Jay glanced aside enough to recognize Eddie. Relief surged through him. The treachery of the parking lot might have kept him in the church building doing odd jobs until the Municipal Road Crew—that is to say, the sun—had gotten to work.

Mrs. D. turned to see who'd stepped in, then gasped. "Oh, how sweet!"

It took Jay a moment to realize she wasn't talking about Eddie, but rather about the halo-haired boy by

Eddie's side. Mrs. D. was kneeling in front of Jamie with her hands on his shoulders. "What a doll! I didn't see him at the Caf yesterday." She turned to Jay. "He reminds me so much of my grandson when he was this age."

Jamie was looking at the woman with a hungry curiosity.

Jay said, "Jamie, meet Mrs. D. She's the woman who cooked the meal in the cafeteria yesterday, and today she brought cookies for you and all the other boys upstairs."

"Maria too?" said Jamie.

"Yes, her too."

Mrs. D. said, "He's so young. Those two kids with the rolls yesterday are his brother and sister?" She paused. "Is the little girl okay in with all those boys?"

"Maria smacked around two of them the first night for swiping her pillow, so she's got their respect. I'm not sure what their situation was. I'm told it was pretty drastic."

"Oh, what a shame." She tried to straighten the boy's too-small coat, then sighed. "How awful for you to have to be here, and so young." Standing, she turned to Father Jay. "Well, time to get the day started."

"It's already begun," Jay said with a chuckle. "Thanks for the cookies."

Eddie waited almost until the woman had left before adding his own, "Thank you." Jamie just watched the woman leave without saying a word.

Kevin and Bill responded to a call at a park due to some noisy teenagers. The kids all hastily extinguished cigarettes as the cops approached--and they really were "kids". Thirteen or fourteen years old, hooded sweatshirts instead of winter jackets, bushy hair down to their chins on the guys and past their shoulder blades for the girls.

Bill handled it all, Kevin silent and imposing behind him. The kids claimed they hadn't been making much noise at all, other than a couple—maybe just a few—shrieks during a snowball fight. And they'd been breaking ice sheets off the playground equipment, maybe throwing just a little bit of it—

Kevin had heard it all before. Normal kids having normal fun, a little old lady irritated that she was able to hear them from within her house just beside her window if she turned off the television and listened hard with her ear pressed to the glass—and how dare those kids throw snow? Someone could get hurt. Time to call the cops.

The kids agreed not to smoke any longer (yeah, right) and promised not to make any more noise (at least for fifteen minutes) and the officers turned to leave.

As they trekked out of the park, Kevin stopped in front of a hump of ice-covered snow.

It stood about waist-high, about as wide around as it was tall. "They have boulders in this park?"

"Not last time I was here."

Someone could have hauled in a boulder, but it was unlikely. "What on earth is this?" Dear heaven, not a frozen homeless man, huddled under a blanket like an Eskimo in his igloo.

Kevin brushed off the tip, and with a crack some of the ice came away, bringing needles with it.

"Holy cow! That's a pine tree."

Bill huffed. "I didn't know they could bend like that."

Kevin brushed it again, revealing more branches. He realized the kids were watching, and Bill was watching too, but he kept pushing the snow off the lump of bent tree. Armfuls of icy snow came off, and at any moment he expected the tree to snap upright, released from the weight. Instead it only rose a little taller.

Bill joined him. Together, the two police officers shook the branches loose, excavating the trapped branches underfoot, and making the tree taller and taller. Maybe it had stood six feet without the snow, but now it was almost four feet, and its head remained bent.

"Do you think it can survive this way?"

"I have no idea." Bill shrugged. "I took criminal justice, not botany."

"But the trunk isn't snapped."

"Well, remember that blizzard last year? The chief said the most flexible trees survive the worst ice storms." Bill began digging around the base now, releasing the trapped branches from the standing snow. "Either they've got to be so strong that nothing can take them down, or they have to be able to bend when it comes."

"This is crazy, though."

Kevin looked up to find the kids all standing around him.

"Whatcha doing?" one said.

"This is a tree. Recognize it?" Bill grinned. "We're the city's finest. We'll help anyone."

One of the girls moved in to help dig.

Bill and Kevin were beaded with ice chips. Kevin dusted his gloves against one another. The highest point of the tree had reached about five feet, and still the crown had risen only knee-high off the ground. As the teenagers set to work, Kevin and Bill stepped back.

"We could leave." Kevin couldn't take his eyes off the tree as the kids pulled every bit of ice off all of the branches, circling like a triage team, shouting instructions. They were actually more organized than some ambulance corps he'd worked with. That little old lady would call back to report them again if she had her television off. ("9-1-1? There are some kids digging out a tree--and two armed men making them do it! Send a whole squadron!")

Bill had a faint smile. "We can stay."

"Hey!" One of the kids laughed. "The ground is totally bare under here!"

"It's like a neat home for a squirrel."

"I bet something could hide from the storm under here!"

Kevin stepped back and regarded the tree for a long moment. By now it stood about eight feet tall, so he had to pull his head back to see the crown. Although it stood bent a little, it had straightened as much as it could for the moment.

"You were right." Bill rubbed his gloved hands together. "That tree was going to stand tall again."

Chills shot up Kevin's back, and not just from having his boots in the snow. He looked at Bill, but he didn't say anything.

As they rode in the patrol car, Kevin stayed wrapped in his own thoughts. It just seemed too...too strange. Too coincidental. Hadn't he told Jay that someone bent double by tragedy could never stand straight again? And there before him, a tree crushed by ice had risen out of the ground as if from the dead.

What could it be if not coincidence? Did God exist? Was God answering Jay's prayers just to string them both along, the better to laugh in their faces later? Did Jay have so much belief that he'd rearranged the world? It was quantum theory or something—someone wanted something so much, or could visualize it so clearly that the thing had no choice other than to happen. It didn't make sense any other way. Jay with his will that could bend iron bars had bent the laws of the universe, bent that tree, and placed it just where Kevin would find it.

But that meant Kevin had brushed the ice off the tree while in thrall to Jay's will. That made no sense either. And had the kids said what they did under Jay's spell? For once, it made more sense to believe it was an act of God.

Jay would say—if Kevin cared to mention it to Jay at all—Jay would say that God wanted to "make nice" with him, or that God had shown He cared.

But what about all of the times God had shown He didn't care? Was one straightened tree supposed to undo all the hatred Kevin had seen? What about all the broken trees? What about all the pain, all the waste, all the useless losses?

No one gets a second chance. Even if a tree got a second chance, what about all of the people snuffed out like a candle? What about that girl who had died two years ago on Christmas Eve?

Kevin folded his arms as another call came in, reaching for the radio to respond even as Bill turned on the sirens to speed across a city where a man got only one chance.

Ten

The remainder of Jay's day blurred together on "fast-forward." The sun burned off the ice; parish volunteers arrived to decorate the church; more parishioners brought gifts or holiday goodies; the boys upstairs devoured one hour of Mrs. D's baking in five minutes; and Jay made final phone calls, pleas, and threats to get everything ready for Christmas.

In the kitchen alongside the Caf, he opened the refrigerator to pull out one of the bowls, and his hands hit the top of the bowl. He paused. *What the—?*

He tapped it again, then winced, remembering the frozen holy water. The refrigerator was freezing things. Just what he needed, for the refrigerator to die on Christmas Eve.

Mrs. D. said, "Something the matter, Father?"

"The fridge—" as he was saying it, he paused, then touched the bowl again and realized the top of the bowl was covered with saran wrap. "Oh. Never mind."

She chuckled. "One of those days?"

"Is Christmas Eve *allowed* to be one of those days?"

"I don't see why not," said Mrs. D. "It's a day."

Kevin and Bill booked someone for shoplifting ("Even Santa Claus has to pay the elves, buddy"), and while Bill filled out the paperwork, the desk sergeant waved Kevin over.

Turning, Kevin recognized the woman standing at the desk and took a step backward.

A whine built in his ears. White porch lights. Broken glass. An L-shaped Camry beside a flipped Ford Taurus.

"Officer Farrell?" She reached out to shake his hand. "You probably don't remember me, but I'm Sherry Daniels."

He conveyed to her that he did indeed remember who she was, and again offered his condolences on the death of her daughter two years ago.

She looked misty for a moment, and her gaze dropped. "Christmas won't ever be the same."

He swallowed. "I don't suppose it ever will."

Other than repeating, "I'm terribly sorry," Kevin couldn't think of a thing to say, so he remained quiet.

Mrs. Daniels forced a smile. "That wasn't why I came of course. I didn't mean to upset you." She reached into the shopping bag resting on her arm and pulled out a red box done up with white tissue paper. "I actually came to say thank you."

Kevin blinked. Thank you for telling a woman her daughter was dead?

She put the box into his hands. "I know that can't have been the easiest part of your job, and I'm afraid I wasn't very polite. But you were so calm, so strong, that it made it seem as if everything was going to be fine."

Kevin managed to say he hadn't done all that much, but she wouldn't let him demur. "And then last year you remembered us on Christmas, when it was so awful on the anniversary. No one wanted to even mention her. I'd gone to the cemetery because I didn't know what else to do with myself, and I came home to find you'd been there." She smiled, her eyes careworn. "Just when it felt as if everyone had forgotten, you remembered."

Very aware of the desk sergeant listening, Kevin tried to steady himself. "You're a very strong person."

"No," she said, "it's God who's been strong for me and so good to me. And the first way God was good to me in all this was by sending you to help me that night. I thank God for sending you." She gave him a hug. "And all I could do was give you cookies."

After Mrs. Daniels left, Kevin opened the box to find home-made chocolate chip and sugar cookies. He took a few for himself and left the rest on the sergeant's desk for the other officers. The bounty wouldn't last ten minutes, but that was okay. He wouldn't have to think about them again. He fled to the locker room.

I thank God for sending you.

Can someone bent double by tragedy ever stand straight again?

Between two long rows of lockers, Bill approached him, munching a cookie. "These are pretty good. Whoever brought them, you need to write her one heck of a thank you note."

Kevin tried to sound amused. "She brought them to me as a thank you. Where would it end?"

"No kidding?" Bill tried his lock, found it resisted his tug, then tried it again. It clunked open. He pulled out a bottle of water, but Kevin still hadn't replied. "What was she thanking you for? You found her purse?"

In a flat voice: "I told her that her daughter was dead."

"Ouch." Bill looked at Kevin with intent. "Really?"

Kevin slammed his locker. "You think I make up garbage like that? Two years ago on Christmas Eve, her daughter died in a car crash, and I was the poor slob who walked up her front steps and rang her doorbell. So she thanked God it was me and brought me cookies. I guess I did a better job of it than she expected from the city's finest."

"She thanked God you were the one who brought her bad news?" Bill looked puzzled. "Did she say why?"

You were so calm, so strong, that it made it seem as if everything was going to be all right.

"No," Kevin said. "Not really." He looked down. "No."

Later in the patrol car, Kevin said, "She said I made it seem like everything would be okay."

"Woah." Bill's mouth twitched. "Maybe you did."

"Maybe that woman shouldn't have died."

"I don't doubt it." Bill sighed. "Most of the things we see on the job shouldn't have happened. That's why people need cops. Then the dispatcher sends you."

Kevin frowned. "You saying God's a dispatcher?"

"People screw up. He's got to send someone." Bill tilted his head. "An awful lot of people think He sent them your brother. Maybe this one time, He sent you instead."

I thank God for sending you.

Kevin said, "Why?"

"Because for whatever reason, she needed *you*, the way you say things, the way you made it seem like someone was in control. Maybe you did something in a way that no one else could have." Bill puzzled for a moment. "And maybe because God knew she was the kind of person who would say thank you, and you needed a thank-you."

Mrs. Daniels, baking cookies: *It's God who's been strong for me and so good to me.*

Kevin said in a low voice, "Why would God care?"

They pulled onto the main strip only to get stuck at a red light. Bill finally said, "Because that's the second biggest gift God gave us. First God gave us Himself, but after that, God gives us each other."

Jay with eyes afire: "God gave me a second chance. Are you jealous?"

"And second chances," Kevin murmured.

"And third and fourth chances too." Bill took a deep breath. "I guess the question left for you, Farrell, is whether you're willing to do the same for God." The light changed, but Bill didn't hit the gas yet. He met Kevin's eyes. "Are you willing to give a second chance to God?"

Eleven

*B*y five o'clock, the sun had set. Jay found his coat by feel, a black wool coat with sailor buttons big enough for his fingers to slip through the holes even if he were trembling.

He'd prayed not to have a white Christmas this year. Everyone built up the beauty of a snow-covered December 25th, but Jay felt secretly glad whenever it came merely grey. Snow made life hard for the homeless and added so little to the holiday. Plus, snow made it harder for him to walk.

Eddie would have accompanied him if Jay had asked, but Jay craved silence, a silence Eddie would have tried to fill. *Is that selfish of me?* he asked God.

Jay stepped outside, and the cold surrounded him, stealing his breath.

A block from the church, you couldn't tell the church was even there. Row houses stood in an unbroken line from end to end of the street, the sidewalk parted regularly by two driveways and then two parking spaces. Jay knew the route well, knew where each tree root bumped up the sidewalk and where each square of concrete yawned with cracked stone. Trash sat sodden at the curbside. As he walked, Jay hunched in his coat and pushed his hands deeper into his pockets for the warmth. The blocks went on this way for a mile. When he wanted something different, he'd turn left and walk one block to the main strip.

People passed without saying hello. It was just as well.

Kevin—what to do about Kevin; angry Kevin; Kevin who was too antagonistic toward God ever to be a real atheist. There was no way that divide couldn't hurt their brotherhood, no way at all. Jay dealt with angry ex-Christians on a daily basis, but dealing with Kevin—it was different because Kevin thought Jay was wasting his life.

Jay tried to turn it around. How would he himself cope if he believed all cops were deluded and prejudiced, and that the criminals were right? Jay couldn't begin to form the arguments against the police force, though, so he tried instead to change his brother's role in the hypothetical story. What if his brother were a practicing Satanist? Well, that involved hurting people or animals. What if his brother were—

—*were so antagonistic toward religion that he couldn't talk about it?*

It might have been the voice of God. Jay thought back, *Ha-ha.*

But maybe it was the same thing. They had a hard time relating—mutually—but Jay at least tried to understand. Kevin only mocked him. If Kevin knew that he prayed for him, Jay wondered, would that seem like mockery too?

Oh, that would be bad. He'd better keep that under his hat in the future. *I don't want to be one of those people who uses Your name as a weapon.*

Of course, God knew what he prayed in secret. Kevin didn't need to know in the first place. But it made things awkward, as if Jay were involved in a sordid affair he needed to hide from his own family.

An SUV laid on the horn as it blew through an intersection. Nasty shouts volleyed back from another driver. The boom of a passing stereo grew distorted as it drew away. And always in the background, Jay heard the indistinct noises of a city in preparation.

Why had Kevin turned on him? All those years as kids, finding trouble when they could, making trouble when they couldn't, Kevin had been always ready for Jay's next escapade. At night, Jay had lain flat on his back in bed, eyes open in the dark as he tried to think of the next mischief that would leave Kevin grinning for days.

Where'd that all go? he asked God. *Where's my little brother?*

When he'd joined the army, he'd half expected Kevin would enlist the next year.

Jay turned at the corner and walked toward the sounds of the highway sunken through the center of the city. Five minutes later he stood on the overpass, cars rolling both beneath his feet and behind his back. The ones below on the highway moved more slowly than the ones at street level. A long column of red lights brightened, dimmed, jerked forward, and then brightened again. Typical traffic jam. Jay was sometimes glad he couldn't drive any longer because it was spiritually better for him not to be trapped in that kind of morass: less temptation to wrath. The traffic in the other direction flowed heavy with white lights, but at least it moved.

For a few minutes, Jay stood leaning on the railway. The air stank of exhaust, and the cars made sluicing sound as they rolled through the slurry in the streets.

What's getting to Kevin, anyhow? He's so much angrier than he was a few years ago. Is it the job? He sees the worst part of people. Although I guess I do too—the scammers, the lazy folks who want charity and sympathy in exchange for nothing at all. The difference is that Kevin sees all the bad and none of the good. I get to see the heart of people too in my vocation.

But did Kevin really see only the bad? Didn't he ever get the good things, like people turning in lost wallets or people helping one another after a disaster?

Kevin once laughed and said, "No, they don't call us for those things."

Jay didn't know—and wouldn't ask—if his brother had ever shot someone. Not Kevin, please not Kevin. Jay himself had shot people, but he didn't want to think about those days. He'd defended the country just as his brother defended the city, hardly a sin, but during dark nights Jay wondered if he'd killed anyone, if anyone had gone home as wounded as he had, if anyone cursed the American soldier who had squeezed off that shot.

God, forgive me. It wasn't sinful to have done whatever he had in the line of duty. But it didn't always feel that way.

He looked the rest of the way across the overpass. The brightest lights were the orange and yellow logo of the neighborhood supermarket, Soucy's. Like all the supermarkets in the city, it was open now and would be open until noon tomorrow for those last-minute forgotten items, the quick run-through for milk or a greeting card.

He'd stopped by there already. The store manager had said no, they couldn't take Eddie. And no, he wouldn't reconsider.

"Father Jay?"

Jay turned toward a man's voice.

"Father," said the speaker, "it's too cold to be standing out here. Do you want a lift?"

"No thanks. I'm clearing my head before the evening services."

The person sounded familiar enough to be a parishioner, but he wasn't fully visible in the dark. "You should be wearing your gloves."

Jay chuckled. "I work for Saint Gus. I can't afford gloves."

A moment later he felt the person handing him a pair. "Here. Take mine."

"I can't—"

"I've got more. Don't worry." The person continued walking away. "Have a good Christmas!"

"I will. Thanks for the gloves." Jay couldn't see the person any longer, but he knew he hadn't turned around as he left. Jay still had no idea who it was or if the person really had another pair.

The red and white lights beneath his feet continued flowing, and Jay pulled the gloves on his hands. He lingered a long time before taking a step back to the rectory, one gloved hand trailing the steel guardrail on the overpass.

But then he turned, and with a deep breath, he once again approached the supermarket.

The call came over the radio at around eleven o'clock. "Assault in progress at the Central Mall."

Bill put on the lights and sirens and banged a U-turn. Kevin grabbed the radio. "We're headed in. Give us a description of the perp."

The dispatcher audibly hesitated. "It's— it's Santa Claus."

Bill roared with laughter.

Kevin said, "Repeat that?"

"It's Santa Claus. Two of them in a fist fight at the mall entrance."

"Don't go off the road!" Kevin said. Bill was laughing so hard he was gasping.

They arrived at the mall to find three other cop cars and four cops plus mall security doing their best to keep the Santa Clauses away from one another.

A sergeant approached. "It's just about over. They're bell-ringers for different charities, and they wanted the same spot."

Crowds of final-hour shoppers stood gawking as the police cuffed the two Santas, but then they complained that they didn't have enough time to stick around to give statements. One of the Santas had a bloody nose. The second was holding his arm to his side and threatening to sue the other Santa, the other Santa's charity, the police, the mall, and the city government.

Bill muttered, "Maybe he can sue God too while he's at it."

"So, about this 'Peace of Christ'...?"

"These guys represent Christ the same way the New England Patriots represent Democracy."

The sergeant said, "You two take one of them to the station. We can't put them both in the same car. Much as I'd like to."

"Do I get to fill out the paperwork?" said Bill. "Because damn, I've always wanted to put Santa's name on a booking sheet. Known aliases: Kris Kringle, Saint Nick. The whole works."

The sergeant rolled his eyes. "Do it, and then you can go home for the rest of the night."

"Sounds good to me." Bill grabbed Broken-Arm-I'll-Sue and maneuvered him into the back seat. Kevin radioed that they were coming in while Bill filled in the log book. It took ten minutes to escape the jammed parking lot, navigating between parking space seekers.

"I'd love to turn on the siren right about now."

"Don't tempt me." Bill finally pulled out onto the circumference. "This place is a zoo."

The Santa in back said, "I'm gonna sue—"

"Sure you are. My name's Bill Brooks. Be sure to name me as a defendant."

Kevin chuckled. "So how do you figure this adds to the Christmas cheer, man?"

"It doesn't. But this isn't Christmas, not really. This is greed dressed up, just the way someone letting his kid toss a nickel into the bell-ringer's pot isn't charity as much as it's cheap entertainment for the kid."

Kevin glanced at Santa. "So what is Christmas, then?"

"It's the way you took this shift so someone with a family could be home with his kids, or the way your brother slaves year-round to make sure those folks at his church have a decent meal. It's the way the people at St. Gus pulled together to find jobs for those troublemaker boys upstairs." Bill grinned. "You see the TV specials and it's about doing something special on that day because it's Jesus's birthday. That's garbage. I think it's more like you act on Christmas the way you acted the rest of the year, plus one. It's not magic. It's habit."

Kevin watched the streetlights as they passed in uniform rhythm over the patrol car rolling along the avenue. "People feel worse at this time of year over normal things."

"I know." Bill sighed. "They show us all these perfect holidays on TV and in the books, and who really has that? We're just people, and people aren't perfect. Sometimes it's the surprises that mean the most to us, the thing we didn't expect we'd like but ended up loving best. Or the way we said thank you for that scratchy sweater in five shades of ugly and made an old relative happy. Those are the gifts that make us bigger instead of smaller."

Santa piped up, "You guys are what, philosophy cops?"

"The way you're the Boxing Santa, yeah." Kevin chuckled. "And where would God fit in all this?"

"I don't think He really does any longer." Bill frowned. "It's hard to mix in the presents with His Presence. If you know what I mean. But He's definitely here. You just have to look harder."

"Where?" Kevin said.

"I'd start with your brother's church." He glanced sidelong at Kevin. "You gotta go talk to him eventually, you know. You might as well do it tonight and tell him it's your Christmas gift."

Twelve

Midnight Mass was Jay's second-favorite service of the year. Easter Vigil was unparalleled, as far as he was concerned, in terms of sheer power, but Midnight Mass had a splendor entirely different. He reveled in the sparkle brought to life by a frigid night, parishioners outwardly tired and inwardly excited, children vibrating with anticipation, and a sense of connection to mysteries almost ancient. As he lit the white candle in the Advent wreath, the awe of the moment left him breathless.

After the Mass, the parishioners of St. Gus held an all-night party in the church basement, lasting from the end of Midnight Mass to the beginning of the sunrise service on Christmas morning. Jay had suggested it for Easter Sunday his first year, and the parish had all but demanded one for Christmas as well. Parishioners provided potluck dishes and still more plates of cookies, pies, and candies. Someone turned on the coffee urns with enough coffee to keep the entire parish awake until sunrise. The coffee became progressively stronger as it boiled down through the small hours of the morning.

The choir commandeered one of the corners and started jamming with a few of the youth group's amateur guitar players.

Mrs. D. wheeled out a television and then called over the boys from upstairs. "I heard someone wanted Christmas specials," she began, and no one heard any more as the kids mobbed her demanding their favorites. After many threats, shouts and insults, a selection was made—the rest stacked in careful order to insure a full night of television.

Jay joined the choir and contributed his bass. Then some of the younger kids sang a couple of the more popular songs playing on the radio, and Jay sat with them listening and every so often wincing at the lyrics.

Nick came up to him, smelling vaguely of buttered popcorn, but didn't say anything.

Jay said, "Are you having a good time?"

Nick grunted, then handed Jay a paper cup. It felt warm against his palm, and light enough that Jay explored the top with his fingers. Popcorn. "Thanks."

"It's nothing."

The choir launched into "The Little Drummer Boy," and Jay sang along with them, doing the bass "rum...pa pum" part like a big drum. Nick didn't leave his side. At the end, after the little boy "played his best for him," Nick started to walk away.

Then he smiled at me. Parum-pa-pum-pumm. Me and my drum.

Nick pivoted and returned as the song ended. He folded his arms and turned his back to Jay, then said, "So, uh, why are you doing all this?"

Jay grinned. He couldn't help it.

At two o'clock in the morning, Santa made a surprise visit, distributing candy canes. No one was more surprised than Jay, since he hadn't made any arrangements for this. It wasn't until he got close enough to hear Santa's voice that he realized the man wearing the suit had come from his own family tree rather than the North Pole.

Jay shook Santa's hand. "You're a lunatic."

"Thanks." Kevin didn't let go, then tugged Jay's arm so he stepped closer. "I've been a real idiot."

Jay gave a relieved smile. "Tell me something I didn't know."

"I'm trying to apologize here."

"Save it." Jay gave Kevin a hug. "I'm just glad you're back. We can talk about it later." He paused. "Why *are* you here?"

"We booked a guy who didn't need this suit any longer, and I figured if the suit fit, I'd wear it."

Jay grinned. "Thanks. The kids are getting a kick out of it."

Starving sharks in a frenzy would have stared in awe of the kids swarming Santa to get gifts and make requests. Jay backed off to watch his brother defend himself as only Santa can: with plenty of Ho-ho-hos and candy canes. There were photographs and even some of the adults sat on Santa's lap with requests of their own.

He'd never thought of his brother as good with kids. He didn't know Kevin even liked kids. But here they were, clambering all over him, begging and exhibiting simultaneously their cutest and most obnoxious behaviors. Kevin was laughing with them, talking, encouraging, and showing them a good time. In a way, it reminded Jay of when he and Kevin used to tussle: they'd fight to the death with each other, but let an outsider try to interfere and instantly they'd unite.

Eventually Santa announced that he needed a break, and Mrs. D. herded the swarm back to the television.

"Some kids you've got there," Kevin said to Jay.

"I was wondering whether you'd survive, yeah." He took a breath and looked momentarily cautious. "You kept evading my question before. I thought you were never coming back."

Kevin walked to the far side of the parish hall, his pace modulated so Jay could keep up with him, and then he settled onto a beat-up couch. The worn cushions sagged. Jay laughed. "You didn't realize, but no one can ever climb out of this couch once he sinks in."

"It is pretty old," Kevin admitted. He gestured to the coffee. "I'm being rude, but are you going to drink that?"

Jay handed him the cup. "Remember the time you snuck coffee into the hospital for me?"

"You were off the respirator two days." Kevin laughed. "You needed a reward for continuing to breathe."

"The nurses were so angry, so you promised that mega-sized coffee was all for you."

"And you signed at me *Like hell it is*." Kevin grimaced as he sipped the coffee. "This is an awful trade, though—what I gave you was hot and not burnt."

"I didn't promise it was any good." Jay chuckled. "Okay, later. You go begift the kids, or whatever it is Santa does. I'll be here when you're done."

Holly showed at three a.m.. "Late closing," she told Jay as she pulled off her gloves. "It was positively insane. I got a table of fifteen with only half an hour until closing time." She hesitated. "So, is breaking and entering a sin if Santa Claus does it?"

"You'd have to ask Santa Claus." Jay grinned, not taking the bait. "I'm given to understand he has some law enforcement experience."

Holly followed the direction of Jay's glance, and he caught the moment she recognized Kevin as Santa. The kids were still going to him to have their pictures taken—even the older boys—and Santa still had a few candy canes left in the bag. Jay thought he recognized Jamie climbing onto Santa's lap to ask for a gift, and he didn't envy Kevin that moment. Really, what else could the kid be asking for?

Holly stepped away from Jay, and he let her go. She waited alongside until Kevin saw her during a break in the picture-taking. Gesturing to the kids to wait, Kevin stepped away from the chair and approached Holly.

From across the hall, Jay couldn't hear what was said, nor was his vision good enough to pick up the expressions on their faces, but he could well-imagine both: uneasy, guarded. And yet Kevin would have that earnestness in his eyes, the authority that for some reason only grew more compelling when he questioned himself. Holly? He couldn't begin to guess what she might be thinking, and he said a quick prayer that the Holy Spirit would guide their conversation.

Several of the parishioners had made up gifts for the boys upstairs, and Jay had Santa distribute them. Many of the boys got new clothes. Mrs. D. had purchased eleven matching backpacks of the current cool name-brand (three kid-sized) which the boys universally loved. Some of the Archangels made immediate trade offers.

Jay asked the adults to let the kids come to him. "I hope you're glad for all the loot you've gotten," he began, and the boys cheered. Everyone in the parish hall laughed. "But there's still two more gifts to go." He looked around. "Eddie, can you come up here?"

When Eddie didn't respond at once, the boys pushed him forward.

"Eddie, there's someone who wants to meet you." Jay turned to his left and brought their attention to the owner of the grocery store. "He wants to give you a special Christmas gift."

The man cleared his throat. "I would like to offer you a job."

Jay waited until Eddie realized what he'd been given. When it happened, Eddie's eyes lit up like a

Christmas tree, and his smile took over his whole face. "Really? When can I start? Should I start now?"

There was some general laughter. The man said, "Why don't we wait until the day after Christmas, perhaps?"

Jay turned to his other side. "Mrs. D.?"

Mrs. D. walked forward. Jay said quietly, "Jamie, Maria, and Louis, can you please come here?"

Everyone was quiet. Mrs. D. approached the three children and crouched down before Jamie. "It broke my heart to think of the three of you without a home to go to on Christmas day. I've been enjoying having you around the church so much. You brighten up the day, and you remind me so much of my grandchildren. Would it be all right if you spent some time living with me? I don't have many toys or video tapes, and I don't own any computer games, but I have a warm house and a back yard, and I have neighbors with kids, and I would love to cook for you and share a home with you until your parents are found." She smiled at Jamie, then stood and looked at the other two. "What do you think?"

Jay realized he was holding his breath. He had told her it was entirely up to the children where they stayed.

Louis said, "I think we would like that." Maria beside him only nodded.

Jamie said in almost a whisper, "Can I still see Eddie sometimes?"

Mrs. D. said, "Of course you can. We can walk down to the church every day if you like."

Jay said, "When Eddie's not at work, you mean."

There was relieved laughter all around, and Mrs. D. hugged the children. Jay took a deep breath and sank back into his chair. These all-nighters were fun, but they were also exhausting.

Santa Claus crossed the room and sat beside Jay while the boys stuffed all of their gifts into their new backpacks. As they dispersed, he said, "Their parents may still turn up. They may not be with that woman long."

"If it makes them all happy, it can't hurt even if it's brief. The kids need as much love as they can get." He looked sideways. "You make a good Saint Nick."

"Thanks. I bring my own padding."

"The way you were putting away the cookies before, I thought you were *making* your own padding."

"Very funny. Is ridicule one of the seven deadly sins?"

"Not that I can recall."

"Well, it should be."

One of the parishioners approached Jay and asked if he could bless a rosary for her. She opened a box to reveal a brand new string of fifty-nine wooden beads, plus a silver-toned crucifix and a triangular medal at the center. Jay had her hold it in her palm while he murmured a prayer, and then made the sign of the cross over it. After the woman thanked him, he said, "Pray the first one for me. God knows I need it."

Once she'd gone, Jay laid a hand on Kevin's arm, then turned toward the smudge of light that was his brother's face to his very tired eyes. "Hey, Saint Nicholas? Come with me."

Together they made their way up the creaky back steps to the sacristy behind the altar area of the church. Jay had to take it slow, moving with a mixture of care and pain.

Halfway up, Kevin said, "What was the deal about blessing the rosary?"

Jay spoke between breaths. "Oh, anyone can bless anything, but some people like it more when a priest does it or someone special to them. When we were ordained, the Bishop gave all three of us rosaries blessed by Mother Teresa."

Kevin nodded. "How does it work?"

Jay chuckled. "I'm not quite sure myself. I figure God knows."

Once in the vesting sacristy, Jay flipped on the lights and made his way to a couch upholstered in the best green vinyl the 1970s had to offer.

Kevin glanced at the long rack of altar server robes. "Are you going to induct me into the church to save my filthy hell-bound soul?"

Jay rubbed his forehead thoughtfully. "You said you wanted to talk. So talk to me."

Nearly a minute passed, Kevin standing and Jay sitting in a room permeated by the muted sounds of a Christmas party beneath their feet.

"I'm sorry I didn't respect your beliefs."

Jay frowned. That was an apology, and it was probably even accurate, but it wasn't the point. Kevin had to know that wasn't the point.

After Jay had waited him out, Kevin ran a hand through his hair. "I had you all wrong, you know."

Jay still maintained silence.

Kevin's mouth twitched. "I kept thinking of you as working one hour a week when you had to do your church service. Everyone going around telling you how holy you were and what a higher calling you had while you sat like an executioner passing judgment and telling us we were all going to hell. Quoting scripture rather than thinking. Oh, and asking for money."

Jay said, "That's not really it, is it?"

Kevin frowned. "You're going to be a jerk about this, aren't you?"

Jay's brow furrowed as he nodded. "I don't want to go through this again. Whatever you need to say, I want to hear it. I'm listening."

"I lost everything. We lost mom. We effectively lost Dad after Mom died. It was just us. And then—" Kevin stared at the floor.

"And then you lost me too," Jay said. "You can't be mad at the army, and you can't be mad at Iraq, so you're being mad at God. But aren't you avoiding being mad at the one you should be mad at?"

Kevin shrugged. "I can't be mad at you." He pointed at the Santa suit. "I'm jolly, remember?"

Despite himself, Jay laughed. Kevin did the same, but he walked to the window and stared at the street lights creating yellow circles in the parking lot.

"You and me were all we had," Kevin said. "Now you're running the streets and making mischief with

God, yeah, and that's really annoying. If God doesn't exist, then you ditched me for a phantom. But if God exists, then He could have picked anyone. Why'd He take you?" He turned back to Jay. "I can't fight that. You've made your choice. I should let Him have you."

Jay leaned back on the couch and closed his eyes. "I'd kind of prefer you didn't. God knows how to share. So do I."

Kevin turned from the window, leaning against the wall. "Well, that's pretty much it. I'm not saying I believe in God or believe in the same God you do. But you have this life here, and if you'll still have me in yours, I'm willing to give it a chance." Kevin shook his head. "It's hard to think that my hellion brother went on and became better than me."

"No, not better." Jay sat forward. "Different, not better. You're my hero. There's nothing shameful about that."

Kevin smiled a little. "I got you some paint."

Jay's eyes narrowed. "That's eighty pounds of rice."

"I knew you'd say that. I've also got eighty pounds of rice in my trunk." When Jay laughed, Kevin said, "And I'll help you paint downstairs when the holiday craziness dies down." He studied Jay for a moment. "You look like you're about to pass out. You want me to walk you back home?"

Jay shook his head. "I was planning to crash here for a few hours. There's a Mass at eight. If I'm in the church already, I won't oversleep."

Kevin sighed. "The trick when you're doing a twenty-four hour shift is never to sit down. I'll let you sleep. But—before that..."

Jay squinted at Kevin. "What?"

Kevin swallowed. "I feel silly, but maybe you should bless my badge or something."

Jay burst out laughing. Kevin reddened. "No," Jay said. "I have a better idea. You come here."

With Kevin standing before him, Jay took both his hands and laid them on his head. "Now you bless me."

Kevin jerked away. "What? How do I do that? What do I say?"

Jay paused. "I normally say something like 'I bless you in the name of the Father, the Son and the Holy Spirit.' I guess you wouldn't want to do it that way, though."

"No, I'll say it. It can't hurt." Kevin put his hands back on Jay's head, and Jay felt the warmth of Kevin's hands resting against his hair, a warmth he normally associated with the presence of God. "I bless you in the name of the Father, the Son, and the Holy Spirit."

Jay said, "Amen," and made the sign of the cross.

Kevin crouched beside the couch so he was at eye-level to Jay. "You get some sleep, okay? I'll be back again."

With a grin, Jay said, "You have to be back. You've got my rice," and Kevin laughed.

Jay listened until he heard Kevin leave the church. He laid his head against the green cushion and closed his eyes. *It worked out okay, God,* he thought, but before he could pray more, the last twenty-four hours caught up with him, and he fell asleep. Sometimes, a nap is better than a sack full of toys from Santa Claus.

It was a long Christmas morning, every Mass packed to standing room only, and he spent a long time greeting parishioners. Eddie stayed to help afterward, as if proving himself capable of bagging groceries with the best of men. Mrs. D. collected the three children's scarce belongings while the kids chattered with questions: Was there a tree? Would there be dinner? Did she have a dog?

After the activity subsided, Jay walked alone to the rectory basement for a well-deserved nap. What a good Christmas. The kids had gotten what they needed: tangible signs of love and a little perspective, some food and the knowledge that many people cared about them. *Thank you,* Jay prayed, deeply tired. He sat on his bed, but before he'd stretched out he saw something white with a splash of red on his desk.

Only when he got closer did Jay realize what it was, and he laughed out loud. Standing on his desk, adorned with a simple ribbon bow, was an electric can opener.

Epilogue

"And this is the tree."

Holly stepped back to study the pine. It stood higher than both their heads, and when she turned, she found Kevin admiring it too. The tree bent somewhat from its time beneath the ice, but still it stood alive and healthy, growing, needles extended to the sun. "How do you feel? You're the tree's hero."

"I should have got Cop of the Month for this." Kevin grinned. "Instead they gave it to that guy who pulled two kids out of a wreck on the expressway."

"You've been robbed." Holly chuckled. "They could at least award you the Tree Surgeon's Citation of Excellence."

"Not too loud. They might institute one." Kevin shrugged. "I just thought since we were passing through, I might as well show you."

"I'm glad you did." Holly slipped her hand into Kevin's and gave a squeeze. "Thanks."

Kevin checked his watch. "We'd better get moving if we want dinner before the movie. Come on."

Holly glanced once move over her shoulder as they left the park, looking at the tree, grateful for second chances.

Thank you so much for reading *The Boys Upstairs*!

Please consider leaving a review at Amazon or Goodreads (or both.) Forget what your 4th grade teacher told you about book reports: a review can be just a couple of sentences, and authors will love you for it. (Particularly this one.)

If you liked reading about Jay and Kevin, please check out my other books.

If you'd like to hear from me when new books appear, you can check the box at my amazon central page or feel free to email me at JaneLebak@gmail.com. I've also got a Facebook page at http://www.facebook.com/JaneLebakAuthor.

Thanks again for reading my story, and I hope to hear from you.

Made in the USA
Lexington, KY
06 December 2015